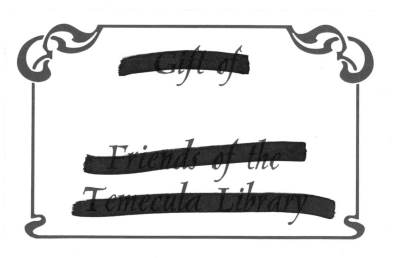

Beautiful Girls

Stories by

Beth Ann Bauman

MacAdam/Cage Publishing
155 Sansome Street, Suite 550
San Francisco, CA 94104
www.macadamcage.com
Copyright © 2002 by Beth Ann Bauman
ALL RIGHTS RESERVED

Library of Congress Cataloging-in-Publication Data

Bauman, Beth Ann, 1964—
Beautiful girls / by Beth Ann Bauman.
p. cm.
ISBN 1-931561-35-4 (Hardcover : alk. paper)
1. Women—Fiction. 2. Girls—Fiction. I. Title.
PS3602.A95 B43 2003
813'.6—dc21

                                                    2002153548

Excerpt from "Memory" from *The Book of Images* by Rainer
Maria Rilke, translated by Edward Snow. Translation copyright
© 1991 by Edward Snow. Reprinted by permission of North Point
Press, a division of Farrar, Straus and Giroux, LLC.

"Stew" was originally printed in *Literal Latté*
"The Middle of the Night" appeared in *Many Lights in Many
Windows: Twenty Years of Great Fiction and Poetry from The
Writers Community*.

Manufactured in the United States of America
10 9 8 7 6 5 4 3 2 1

Book design by Dorothy Carico Smith.

Beautiful Girls

Stories by

Beth Ann Bauman

MacAdam/Cage

Judy, Dedy, Debby & Sandy

to girlhood

*And you wait, await the one thing
that will infinitely increase your life;
the gigantic, the stupendous,
the awakening of stones,
depths turned round toward you.*

—Rainer Maria Rilke
translated by Edward Snow

CONTENTS

THE MIDDLE OF THE NIGHT

ALLIE'S FATHER IS ASLEEP BENEATH THE AZALEA BUSH.
Allie stands on the lawn, barefoot, in her nightgown,
watching him breathe. His open mouth vibrates. She
plucks a flower off the bush, drops it over him, and
watches it bounce off his chin and land on his chest.
She kicks him. He doesn't stir.

A breeze lifts Allie's nightgown, making her shiver.
This is the middle of the night, she thinks. She's never
seen the middle of the night. She darts across the
moist lawn, quickly, in a rush of glee. She leaps with
her arms outstretched. Then she runs in figure eights
until she tumbles to the ground and lies on her back,
panting. It is so quiet. Every house is dark except for
theirs, which is lit from basement to attic. The stars
look icy and far away. Lifting her arm, Allie covers a

handful of the sky. The phone rings and she runs inside.

"Hello," she says.

"You sound little," the voice says.

"I'm not."

"How old are you?"

"Eight."

"Are you your father's child?"

"Who is this?" Allie asks.

"I'm the woman your father shtups. Do you know what that means?"

"No," Allie says, leaning against the counter.

"Where is your father, sweets?"

"He's busy and can't come to the phone right now."

"Well, I really didn't want to talk to him anyhow. I think I like you better."

Allie climbs up on the counter, shivering. A breeze blows through the front screen and out the back. Papers on the desk flutter. Allie lunges for a vase of shriveled roses and catches it before it falls.

"What's your father doing?" the woman asks.

"Sleeping."

"With your mother?"

"No..." Allie jumps off the counter.

"I didn't think so."

Last week Allie's father staggered up the drive-way with the weed whacker, singing the New Year's

Eve song. Allie's mother fell to her knees, announced it was the last straw, and said, "How could you sever the heads of my petunias?" Her mother then drew the shades and climbed into bed with a cool washcloth on her forehead. Allie made her mother a Harvey Wallbanger just the way she liked it—a splash of orange juice and Galliano over a tall glass of vodka and ice. But her mother groaned, "I'm on the wagon for good, darling," and she made Allie flush the Harvey Wallbanger in the upstairs bathroom.

"I knew that union was doomed from the beginning," the stranger now says. "I bet you live in a real nuthouse."

"Are you my father's friend?"

"Well, yes and no."

"I'm going to hang up. Goodbye." Allie hangs up. She runs outside, taking a leaping jump off the porch. She runs in circles past her sleeping father and gallops from one end of the lawn to the other.

Allie sleeps late. Outside it is already hot. She walks sleepily into the hallway, feeling crabby and wanting to crawl back into bed.

Yesterday Allie watched as her mother moved into the attic. Her mother, pale, with hair springing out of her bun, pulled down the hatch in the upstairs hallway, and the tiny set of stairs tumbled to the floor. She raced up and down those stairs, carrying a thermos, a sleeping bag, pillows, bananas. Like a squirrel, Allie thought, storing nuts for the winter. "I'm going to live up here for a very short while," her mother said, rushing down the little stairs, blowing her nose.

Allie watched quietly.

"I need to gather my wits," her mother said with wet eyes. She lit the flame in the lantern and hurried to the top of the tiny stairs and climbed into the hole. She blew a kiss. The yellow light illuminated the blackness behind her. "Do you have anything to say to me?" she asked.

Allie sensed something final and desperate in her mother's ghostly face and with a shaky voice said, "I've been to Mount Rushmore and when I looked at the presidents' stone heads I could see their greatness."

Her mother blinked, but gave Allie a quick smile. Then she pulled up the hatch, and the tiny set of stairs folded back in.

This is Allie's interesting sentence and before that moment she hadn't had an occasion to use it. Her second-grade teacher had once wanted an interesting sentence, and at the time Allie couldn't think of one. Her teacher had said children without imaginations were guilty of sloth and headed for a life of despair.

Now Allie stares up at the hatch. She pictures her mother eating a banana in that spooky light. There are bugs up there and spider webs. Her mother is frightening her. How long is a very short while? Allie wonders.

Her father is crumpled in the recliner, looking shrunken, as if his skin is too big for him. He's in the clothes he wore yesterday, and his bare feet are soft and white and thick with blue veins. He smells bad. As Allie sits on the couch, he winks at her. His eyes are wide and alert. "Hey, sleeping beauty," he whispers. There is a twig in his hair. "Your mother wrote you a letter." He hands it to her, but she doesn't take it. Instead, she rests her head on the arm of the couch.

Her father opens the piece of paper with a trembling hand. He winks at her again. The room is bright with sunlight. Allie knows he doesn't feel well. When she closes her eyes she feels an ache behind them.

"Well," he says after a moment. "Maybe we'll read it later." Allie reaches out for the letter, but her father doesn't offer it. "What do you say we go to the grocery store and buy a watermelon?"

Allie doesn't want to go to the grocery store, or anyplace else. She walks over to the window and stands behind the drape. It is hot and quiet in the neighborhood, the kind of day when the cement sidewalk will burn the feet. Later it will cool off. The sun will set and most people will go to bed, but not Allie.

Her father says, "We'll go buy a watermelon a little later, a nice watermelon for the three of us." He

sighs and sinks down into his chair. "Honey, don't
marry someone with a flair for melodrama. Get yourself a straight arrow, a beer drinker." Allie pokes her
head out from behind the drape.

Her father sighs again, running his hand through
his hair. He plucks out the twig, looks at it in a funny
way, and tosses it onto the coffee table. He and Allie
glance away from one another.

Allie came into the world too early. At three
pounds, she fit into the palm of a hand and was hairy
like a monkey. There are many things her parents
have told her that she does not believe and this is one
of them.

Her parents are older than other parents. They
never cook and like to take long drives. They think
Allie should do what she likes, whenever she likes. As
a result Allie is quiet and shy and self-disciplined.

Until recently the three of them would drive to
hotel restaurants or taverns for drinks and finger
food. Often her parents' friends joined them; Allie
didn't like these friends, who always wanted to know
why she was so quiet. "Talk," they would say to her,
but instead she would drink her cherry cola or swirl
the ice in the glass. What did they want to hear, she
wondered. Or they would address her with, "Well,
hello!" as if she was small and in diapers, or one of
them might swing an arm over her shoulders and

confide, "Love is *not* a many-splendored thing. That's a crock of you-know-what."

Allie would then explore the bathrooms, where she would tap-dance on the tile, line up the little soaps, and sit on a lounge chair with her legs crossed, pretending to smoke a cigarette. There were things for her to do in these hotel bathrooms, it was true, even if she did get lonely. But she knew that later she and her parents would snuggle on the couch in front of the TV, her parents peaceful and cheery with liquor, and Allie herself would be happy to be sitting between them, her lids half-closed, on the verge of sleep.

The last time they did anything together was their day trip to Atlantic City to ride in the diving bell. Her father had said beneath the Atlantic was a magical place where sea serpents glided in the waves and where the tentacle of an octopus might wrap around you as a school of stingrays and porpoises swam by. Allie nodded, not quite believing all of it, but liking the part about the stingrays. "Stingrays," she whispered.

"Remember the diving bell from the days of the Steel Pier?" her mother added. "The diving horse? Mr. Salty Peanuts? Oh, those were the days!"

So on a limp, gray day in the spring the three of them climbed into the car and headed for Atlantic City. A fine mist covered them on their walk to the pier, where the diving bell sat bloated and crusted with barnacles. They were the only ones in line. An old man with a hacking cough opened the oval door and said, "Hop in."

Inside smelled unpleasant, like a worn, sweaty shoe. The three of them knelt on the plastic seats with their faces pressed close to the window. Slowly the diving bell was lowered off the pier. They hovered over the water's edge and then with a jolt plunged into the water. Surrounded by a cascade of bubbles, they descended to the bottom of the ocean.

When the bubbles cleared, there was nothing but green murk as far as Allie could see. She waited expectantly for a squid or a shark with many rows of teeth to come gliding by. Kneeling on the bench, Allie waited until her sweaty knees grew stiff, then she crouched on the seat with her forehead against the glass. She imagined that at any moment they would be pulled back to the pier, but they remained in the pulsating, murky water for a very long time, the diving bell making a low hum. "This isn't really the sea," Allie said finally. Her parents continued to stare out the windows, their jaws slack and their skin pasty white.

"Why won't they lift us?" her father asked, unsteadily, licking his lips.

"I don't know," her mother said quietly, opening and snapping shut her purse. Allie's mother's make-up seemed to have melted. Lipstick extended past the border of her lip, and her eyeglasses sat crookedly on her nose.

"I feel sick. You think there's enough air here?" her father asked.

"Stop frightening us," her mother snapped. "Can't we do something?"

"Stop talking." Her father sat very still and moved only his eyes.

"How do you think we get it to go up?" her mother asked in a small, hollow voice.

Allie looked out the window, willing something to happen out there, willing her body to make something happen. Her damp breath steamed up the window.

"Maybe there's a lever or a buzzer or an intercom," her mother nearly shrieked as she turned in a circle inside the diving bell. "Maybe we can find it here, somewhere!"

Her father slumped against the bench, clutching his heart. "Don't use up all the oxygen. Goddamnit," he said.

Allie's mother glared at Allie's father.

Allie took shallow breaths of steamy air. As she looked out the window at the murk, she felt like she'd been had, and the disappointment brought tears to her eyes.

"You're a terrible person in a crisis. Why I married you I'll never know," her mother hissed into her father's ear. She adjusted her glasses on her sweaty face.

"You should have had a martini with lunch,"

Allie's father said in a booming voice. "You're an awful traveling companion when you haven't had a martini with lunch." He stood up, clutched his chest and then sat back down.

"I don't need a martini," her mother said, sadly. "Not now, not ever."

"You do! You do! We all do."

Shaking her head, Allie's mother took off a shoe, stood on the bench, and tapped the top of the diving bell with it.

Huddled together, they were pulled lopsided to the pier. They later learned one of the cables had broken. The local news was there with a camera when the three of them climbed out of the bell, but her parents yanked Allie to the car, and silently they drove home.

Allie bounds down the stairs. Tonight the front and back doors are open, and the house is like a wind tunnel. Her hair blows crazily across her face. It's almost two a.m. She climbs up onto the kitchen counter, but she doesn't see her father in the yard. Then she spots him next door in the Allens' yard, sleeping on a chaise longue. The phone rings.

"Hello."

"Hello, you," the woman says. "Do you feel like blabbing? How would you like to hear about one of the greatest love stories in history? Should I tell you? Let me ask the eight ball." Allie hears a soft glug.

"Should I tell the kid my stories? 'It is decidedly so.' All right."

"Who are you?"

"I'm your father's flame. Your father's a very attractive man but you might not know it by looking at him. We have the kind of love affair where we can't keep our mitts off each other."

"You don't really know my father," Allie says.

"Look, kid—"

"What's your name?" Allie asks.

"Why?" the woman asks. "What's yours?"

Allie stares at her reflection in the oven window. She looks afraid and this frightens her.

"Tell me something. Who do you look like, your mother or father?"

Allie regards her colorless reflection. "I have brown hair, long hair." She inspects her crooked teeth. "I'm in my nightgown. What do you look like?"

"Tell me what you think I look like."

"Ugly."

"Don't get saucy with me, bérnaise." The woman hangs up.

Allie wanders outside. Her nightgown fills with air, making it balloon. The ground is moist beneath her feet. Barefoot, she crosses the street and walks into the Beckers' backyard and touches the roses, which are all in rows by color. The petals are velvety and moist. She picks up a pair of hedge clippers and clips flowers off three of the tallest stems. They fall to her feet.

On a table by the Beckers' pool is a stack of books. One is called *Correct Behavior for All Occasions*. She likes the cover; it pictures a large house filled with silhouettes of delighted-looking people, all with good hairdos, all of them leaning close to one another in cozy, gold-lit rooms.

She wants the book. She wonders if Mrs. Becker will fall to her knees and scream when she sees her beheaded roses. Will Mrs. Becker miss her book?

The sky is filled with bright stars. The wind is crisp. It swishes under Allie's hair onto her bare scalp, filling her with a vibrancy that makes her feel disconnected from the earth, disconnected from the life around her. Crossing the street, Allie hugs the book to her chest.

The next afternoon her father searches for his tooth beneath the recliner—his face is bright red with the strain of bending. Allie reaches her own small hand onto the carpet beneath the chair as she feels for the tooth. Did he have it when he went to sleep last night, she wants to know. He sits back on his heels, cocks his head and smiles sadly at her. "I believe I had a full set then," he says. The dark gap where his front tooth should be makes him look like a stranger to her.

Allie is annoyed and scared that a tooth could just

disappear. It's one thing when you send two socks down the laundry chute and only one comes back, but something very different when you go to bed with a full set of teeth and wake up one short. "Dad!" she shouts.

Her father sticks his finger into the gap, as if the tooth might be there after all, as if it is hiding. "It was a cheap plastic cap," he says. "I should have had it replaced. I've had it since the age of the dinosaurs." He carelessly sweeps his hand over the carpet. "Well, maybe I swallowed it."

"Really?" Allie asks.

"Who knows." He shrugs.

Allie feels like crying. A panic starts thumping through her. What is going on here, she thinks. Today a tooth, tomorrow an ear or a finger.

"Where is it?" she yells.

Her father is looking at her now, but he doesn't seem to see her. Behind her the drapes billow in the breeze—it is a warm summer evening, an ordinary evening. There's the smell of a barbecue not far away.

"Your mother will come back to us, you know. It's like she's on a vacation, honey." He rubs his eyes. "Come sit with me, Allie."

Allie sways from leg to leg. She does not want to sit; she will trace his tracks and find that tooth. "Tell me everywhere you went last night."

On the back porch the world seems much bigger and harder to weed through than it had looked from the living room. Allie will not search for the tooth. How do you find something fingernail-sized out there—where do you start?

Besides, she's lazy during the day. She rests on the sofa, falling in and out of dreamless sleep. Her bones seem to have curved and shifted. She feels like a smaller girl.

She now slumps on the steps, eating potato chips and quietly reciting curses. She waits for the night, when her vision will sharpen, when her energy is up and her spirit yawns and stretches, standing up straight and taking her creaky bones with it.

At midnight it is calm and starry. There is no wind as Allie sits on the front steps blowing bubbles through the wand. The yard is filled with translucent blue bubbles and the low hum of crickets. The phone rings.

"I know it's you," Allie says, picking it up.

"You're a mind reader. How are you, sweets?"

"Good."

"How come I always do all the talking? Lemme ask the eight ball something. Should the kid talk for a change? 'Signs point to yes.' Okay. Act alive; say something."

Allie crunches the phone cord in her hand, thinking fast. "If you had to have a pet snake, a pet rat, or a pet tarantula, which would you have?"

"None! My god! Why would I want one of those things?" The woman is silent for a second. Then she says, "Your problem, kid, is that you take too much crap. You gotta learn to say 'fuck off' once in a while. Don't let anyone push you around. Say it. Say 'fuck off.' For practice."

"Fuck off," Allie says.

"Like you're mad, say it like you're mad."

Allie says it again, louder.

"Try 'go piss up a rope.' Say it with an attitude."

"I like the middle of the night. Do you?"

"What are you interrupting me for? You show a lack of concentration, kid. Your problem—"

Allie hangs up the phone and thinks this is the last straw. She doesn't know what that means, but when she looks at her reflection in the oven window she looks like a person whose feelings have been hurt.

Outside a few fireflies glimmer near the azalea bush. The moon is a toenail clipping, and a breeze blows back her hair.

Allie wanders through the patch of woods behind her house and into the next development. The houses there are dark and quiet. She roams through the backyards like a spirit in a nightgown. On the back stoop of one house a long-necked watering can catches her eye and she waters her feet, leaving wet footprints on the concrete. The back door of the house is open, and Allie peers through the screen down the hallway to where a light shines. She steps inside, imagining a sleeping family there, a mother and father and a few children tucked in their beds. She walks down the hall as though she is invisible.

In the darkened living room a man sits on a couch with a long-haired woman curled up next to him. Soft voices come from a small TV, which gives the room a bluish glow. Both the man and the woman look up at her standing in the doorway.

"Who are you?" the man asks.

"Is that a kid, Marshall?" The woman sneezes three times in a row. "God, I feel like shit," she whispers in a raspy voice. "Am I hallucinating or is that a kid?"

"It's a kid."

The man gently pushes the woman off his lap. Standing, he runs his fingers through his hair as he looks from the woman on the couch to Allie. "This is kind of fucked up," he says.

The woman sneezes again and lets her head fall to the couch. "I must have a fever. Am I a hypochondriac, Marshall?"

"You're allowed," he says. "Where are your parents?" he asks Allie.

Allie leans against the wall. Something smells good in the kitchen, and she looks toward the smell.

"Come here," the man says. He's very tall and slouchy in his body. He's wearing faded jeans and flip-flops.

Allie follows him into the kitchen, where soup boils on the stove. The can says "Chicken & Stars." He stirs it.

"I'm going to walk you home after she eats."

"Oh, I know the way."

"It wasn't a question, it's a statement."

Allie nervously pulls her hair. "Well, goodbye," she says, losing her nerve. As she turns, he grabs her by the back of the nightgown.

"It's two o'clock in the morning. Just hold your horses." He directs her to the stove, where he pours the soup into a bowl. It is steaming hot. He leans over and blows on it. This man smells like grass. "Can you pour that ginger ale into a glass?" he asks.

Allie does. "You want some?" he says. She does not. But as if in a dream she remembers the book with the silhouette people, *Correct Behavior for All Occasions*. In the chapter on food it says to always accept a small offering of food or drink, it's the polite thing to do. Allie takes a glass off the drainboard and pours herself some.

The man takes a box of Saltines down from the cupboard. "Carry the drinks," he says. Together they join the sick woman on the couch.

"Oh, Marshall," the woman says, in a high, pained voice. "I'm all clogged up."

The man sets up the food on a TV tray and puts

his arm around the woman. Her hair is matted, and her face is shiny with sweat. In her feverish daze, she takes delicate sips of the soup.

Allie sips her ginger ale with similar grace.

"Give me something to wrap around my neck. My throat's so sore," she says to Marshall. He puts a sweat-shirt over her and wraps the sleeves around her neck.

"That's much better, Marshall. Much better." She eats steadily, daintily. Looking up at Marshall she says, "You're all right, you know that." Marshall kiss-es her lightly on the forehead.

"What's the kid doing here?" the woman says.

Marshall studies Allie with kind, searching eyes. "What's the deal with you?" he asks.

Allie doesn't know what to say, or what she might say if she could say something. Nothing feels certain to her.

"Do you love each other very much?" Allie asks in a sleepy voice. She asks because she knows what the answer is and wants it confirmed, to know that she's right.

Marshall nods.

Suddenly Allie needs to get home, to check and see that everything is all right there. She's out the back door and into the woods before she realizes no one is following her. She is alone, it is the middle of the night, and her house is not far away.

Her house is dark, even the attic. In the silence

she can tell her father is inside, maybe in the den. Allie stands in the hallway, waiting for her eyes to adjust to the lack of light. The house is very still, there is no movement, no wind, no creaking floors, no life it seems except for her pounding heart, which is too loud to be hers alone and must really be three pounding hearts, the one in the den and the one in the attic and hers here in the hallway.

WASH, RINSE, SPIN

HER FATHER IS SPELLING WITH HIS FINGER. M-O-N and then the rest is gibberish. "Slow down," Libby tells him. He slaps the bed sheets and mimics choking her. Without language he's been reduced to bad acting: smirks, eye rolling, mugging. There's no subtlety; even his eyes are luminous and bald. Some days, like today, he's just too tired to move a pen across paper. He blinks up at her and tries again, slicing his angry finger through the air. "Okay, M-O-N." Her mind is as dull and heavy as a butter knife. "Monkey, monsoon, money."

For a second he looks truly helpless and closes his eyes on her, on everything. From the pillow he offers up a bored, calm face; is this the face he'll wear when he's dead? "Do it again. I'm sorry, Dad." Libby tries a laugh. "Pretty please with sugar on top." She's become a moron.

He continues to ignore her, and in their silence the room is kept alive with sound—the bleep of the heart monitor and the earnest, steady wheeze of the ventilator, poking out of his neck and pushing air into his lungs. Her dad then snaps open his eyes and slowly, as if she is brain-damaged, spells M-O-N-T-H.

"Month, for godsakes," Libby says. He rolls his eyes to the ceiling in exaggerated, delicious contempt. Bad moods now swoop down on him in an instant and leave him puzzled and disheveled, hair poking out, gown slipping off a thin shoulder. But as quick as they come, they leave.

He looks at the slice of sky through the narrow window and patiently starts to mouth something, gesturing with his good hand, the one that isn't large and soft as an inflatable paddle.

"October," Libby says. "It's the middle of October." He raises his eyebrows, surprised. They both stare at the little slice of blue sky—they could be looking into a chlorinated pool. Where has the time gone? Libby wonders. Where has her life gone?

Libby's dad has been in the hospital for weeks. Before then, he had a terrible cough that sounded as if he'd hack up a lung, and even though he spent hours in his garden the sun wouldn't tan him. She remembers visiting one Saturday and watching him

move unsteadily across the yard, his fingers reaching
for the side of the house as the late-day sun cast his
long and crooked shadow. After Labor Day he reluc-
tantly went to the doctor and wound up here in the
CCU. Each afternoon Libby takes the train from
Manhattan, where she lives, to this small tree-lined
town in New Jersey, the same town where she grew
up, although it's no longer familiar.

While her dad sleeps, Libby rests her head
against the chair back and instantly she dreams—
dreams that are filled with unpleasant smells and
involve public transportation. The infectious disease
doctor, who runs, doesn't walk, now flies into the
room, waking her. He makes some preliminary pokes
and prods before pressing his ear to her dad's chest,
as if using the stethoscope would take too long.
Before a question forms in her mind, and she has
many questions, he's gone, out the door.

Milling in the hall is the useless-though-energetic-
and-good-looking oncologist, who won't be treating
the tumor clinging to her dad's lung. This tumor,
which isn't the worst kind, she's been informed,
probably has some relatives that have taken up resi-
dence in his spine or liver. No one knows for sure
since there's nothing to be done. His heart, sorry to
say, simply isn't tough enough. Standing with the
oncologist is her dad's primary physician, a squat,
morose man who delivers all news in the same mon-

otone. Dumpy Downer—Libby's name for him—is looking to wean her father from the ventilator, maybe send him home for a short while, bring in hospice.

Libby eyes a small bag on the nightstand marked "Libby" and realizes it's from one of her dad's girlfriends. Inside is a jelly doughnut, and as she takes a big bite jelly oozes out the side and a glob lands on her suit. She wipes it off, but a dark, glossy stain remains. Something smells funky and she sniffs the air, wondering if it could be her; she can't remember when she last cleaned her five suits.

Libby stands on the platform waiting for the 8:18 to take her back to the city. Tonight her dad asked her to tell his girlfriends, who are actually all ex-girlfriends, not to visit anymore. They talk too much, was how he put it. She told him no. The girlfriends arrive in the mornings, often carpooling together, and stay for hours. They are excellent lip readers, excellent mind readers and excellent at charades. They've acquired the good grace that comes with age. They are a flurry of laughter and perfume. There must be people around him, she reasons to herself. She can't imagine he'll up and die in the face of all this activity. She boards the train and it moves swiftly through suburbia, cutting past trees and highways and people walking their dogs under a pale shine of moon. Libby's head lolls against the dirty window as she fights sleep.

Back in her apartment, she sniffs every suit she owns and dumps them into a pile by the door. Four are food-stained and a fifth has a jagged tear from a barb that pierced through the plastic couch in the CCU waiting room and stabbed her in the thigh. "Dry cleaners," she says aloud. She walks around her apartment in a bra and underwear, watering the brown plants, eating a ham sandwich, and holding counsel with herself. "I want the morphine given every two hours, regardless of whether he asks for it. He's not going to ask until it's too late." She nearly trips over a body bag of laundry in the middle of the floor. "Laundry," she shouts. She's almost out of clean clothes, but there's no time to wash them. How can she be so weary and buzzed at the same time? "How am I coping?" she asks, cupping her face. She tosses herself onto the bed, finishes eating her sand-wich and then curls up under the covers, blowing crumbs toward the wall.

In the morning, she's forced to put on the least sour and wrinkled of the suits, and unfortunately it's the one with the tear in the butt. She stumbles down the stairs with the bag of dirty laundry, the suits piled on top, and lurches up Eighth Avenue to the laun-dromat. The suit on the top of the heap is the color of lime juice. Libby heads for the nearest trash can and dumps it, and she also dumps the purple one with the gold buttons because it too, she realizes for the first time, is butt ugly. Without thinking, she stuffs the remaining suits in with her dirty clothes. At the laundromat Hugh the laundry attendant tosses the bag into a giant bin and tells her it will be ready "pronto tonto."

Libby works at the end of a long wing in the semi-vacant legal department of a large corporation, where the air smells of whiskey and cigars and she has very little to do. Gautreaux, Bilox and Sodder, senior attorneys, arrive late each morning, take three-hour alcoholic lunches and return midafternoon, crocked. Each man weaves toward his office, shuts his door and falls asleep on his respective couch. Gautreaux, the most long-winded of the three, sometimes tells her boring stories after these lunches, always ending with a parable or lesson. "You see, girlie," he'll say, "you see where this is going?" Often he forgets Libby, too, is a lawyer and asks her to water his plants, as he lies helpless and drunken and gurgling on his couch. Once he asked her to call his tailor in Hong Kong and order him another pair of "those natty herringbone trousers."

There are two actual workers, who tirelessly seem to do the work of the whole department: Mr. Muskon and his trusted assistant Miss Perry. Apparently, there once was a departmental secretary, known as Imelda because she was always sneaking off to buy shoes, who disappeared and can't be accounted for.

Acquisition forms arrive midmorning each day in a wire cart pushed by Marianne Switzer. First Bilox, the one with the bowtie, initials the stack, then Libby, Gautreaux, and Sodder. Afterwards, Libby rings Marianne Switzer, who arrives twelve minutes later with her wire cart to whisk the forms to the third floor for further processing. In a nutshell, this is Libby's job. When she asked Gautreaux about more work, he'd said, "All in good time, Pearl." Who was Pearl? She'd started to look for something else, but then her dad got sick, and now she's stuck in her no-job job.

Growing up, Libby's dad had been a good father from a distance. His attention never landed directly on her, but good energy radiated off him in all directions and she felt it as a kind of love.

When Libby was small, her mother's cousin's kid Wilhelmina from New York City spent several summers with them. Wilhelmina was a sour girl, tough as a spike, whose favorite game was Choir Girl, a sadistic version of church in which Wilhelmina would play the plastic organ, and Libby, draped in a sheet and Amish bonnet, would solemnly descend the staircase and make her way behind her father's recliner, which was the pew. When Libby got the speed of her descent right, which wasn't often, they would take communion with the watery scotch left in the bottom of her father's glass. Or if Wilhelmina was feeling chipper, the host might be a gumball, although chewing wasn't allowed. Most times they didn't get to communion because Libby didn't descend the staircase slowly enough, and Wilhelmina would pinch Libby hard, hissing, *"You're not doing it right."*

Once during these church services, Libby's dad reclined in his chair with a copy of the *Tribune* held out in front of him as his bonneted and glum daughter worked her way to and from the pew. Perhaps because Wilhelmina was no relation of his, he caught Libby's eye, pointed to the organ-playing girl, and twirled his finger next to his ear. At this, Libby dove onto his lap while he continued, humming a happy tune, to read the paper. Wilhelmina, sensing a conspiracy, lifted her bony fingers off the keys and glared at them.

Libby's parents divorced when she was twelve, and she divided her time between them, traveling from one end of town to the other with her ratty blue suitcase. Her mother sighed a lot during Libby's teenage years while her dad threw himself into goodwill and charity. Each year he planted an enormous garden and went door-to-door distributing his eggplants and zucchinis, and it was in this way that he met his girlfriends.

All the equipment in the hospital room gives off

a smothering heat that leaves Libby and her dad sticky and soft-brained. A portable fan, precariously balanced atop a garbage can, makes a low, jumbly noise while Libby feeds him ice chips. She's not doling them out fast enough and he snatches the cup, shoveling in three or four chips with his good hand before she grabs it back. "It's gonna go right into your lung and you'll turn blue," she tells him.

"Kiss my ass," he mouths.

"Dad, you can kiss mine."

"Go," he writes. "I'll sleep."

Libby is suddenly so tired, so very tired. She stiffly lowers herself into a chair. Does he really think she can just leave? Each time this happens, she is frightened to think that he might believe she really will leave, that her leaving would be all right with him. She wonders what kind of a life he imagines she has in the city while he is here. "Won't you be lonely without me?" she asks.

"Boring?" he writes. "Hanging out with the old man?"

It's true, dying is boring and tedious among all the other terrible things ascribed to it.

"Boyfriends?" he writes.

"Not at the moment," she says.

"None in this joint," he writes. She frowns. He shrugs with a small smile.

"Pain in the ass," he scribbles on his pad, pointing to himself. She nods. He points to the same words, and then points to Libby. She half-smiles. He writes the word "Talking," circles it, and then draws a diagonal line through it. In solidarity, she zippers her lip.

On TV, Fred Astaire dances across the screen. "Fred again," he mouths. Every time they turn on the TV Fred seems to be swinging around a pole or dipping Ginger. Such poise, such dexterity, such sheer joy. Fred exhausts them. Her dad reaches for her hand and closes his eyes. As he falls asleep, he slides down the pillows and rests lump-like in the middle of the bed. The ventilator keeps a steady, dull rhythm. Something livelier, like a salsa, would better encourage health and healing, she thinks. As he sleeps, his fingers fly up to the ventilator and he wakes. It's been weeks, but he still hasn't gotten used to the tube protruding from his neck. Often he makes like Frankenstein's monster, jutting his arms out in front of him, widening his eyes and letting his mouth go slack. "Your kind of poison," he once scribbled on a pad.

"Not anymore," she'd snapped.

Before her no-job job, and before law school, Libby worked on the production crew of low-budget horror/sci-fi movies that went straight to video. The actors were snarly and unprofessional, the pay was crap and the hours spilled into each other, leaving her with no time for a life. They often shot several movies at once, and in holding at any given time there might have been a group of corpses playing poker, assorted fanged creatures complaining about the air-conditioning, and gross-out, flesh-eating lumps chowing down on meatball heroes. Libby raced from set to set, where several times a day she'd get chewed out for not doing something she hadn't known she was supposed to do in the first place. There were some compensations: Libby, who was never good with clothes, had Jane, her best friend in wardrobe, help her dress when she was dating the cute though underachieving cyclops, Peter. Jane would flip through racks and come up with something chic yet understated, maybe slutty footwear; there was always plenty of this stuff on hand for the hapless heroine whose job was to traipse unwittingly through the cool, serene world before meeting early doom.

One day when none of the bloody corpses was cooperating—one even had the nerve to snap gum while lying on a stone slab under a fake moon—and the director endlessly futzed with the lighting, Libby parked herself behind a tombstone and filled out law school applications.

"But you like the ghoulies," her dad had said.

"I don't."

"Well, all right."

"I'm going to be a lawyer. It's great news, dad."

"I'll say. You can write my will. You get every-

thing. Make sure none of my girlfriends get anything."
Ironically, he is generous to a fault. He bought Geri a
barbecue, Sue an aquarium, and Mary a front-end
loader, even when she had moved to ex-girlfriend sta-
tus. He didn't expect much in return and rarely
phoned the girlfriends. He claimed to hate the phone,
referring to it as the "squawk box," and yet he called
Libby every Saturday without fail.

Early the next morning, Libby puts on a coat over
her bra and underwear and heads to the laundromat,
but Hugh can't find her laundry bag. "It's *huge*,"
Libby says, cornering him by the fabric softener.
"Where could it have gone?" She tries to remember
what was in there—shirts, jeans, fuzzy slippers.

"Man," Hugh says, dejectedly. "I don't know
what to say."

"Find it!" she says, giving him her address.
"Apartment 2G. Two." She holds up two fingers. "G as
in goddamn it."

At home, she pulls out her horror clothes, a speckled mess of paint- and fake-blood-splattered T-shirts
and holey jeans. So comfy, she'd forgotten.

A handsome young kid who reminds Libby of
Neil Lubin, who was supposed to ask her to the prom
but never did, pushes a wire cart down the east wing
as she sits at Imelda's desk. "Filing?" he asks. Libby

gives him her letter to Gautreaux's tailor, requesting
another pair of the size 42 herringbone trousers with
a little more room in the seat, please. The handsome
kid puts it in his empty cart and winks at her before
speeding the single sheet down the hall to the filing
room.

The women's bathroom in the east wing is always
empty, with Imelda gone and Miss Perry not seeming
to have the need, but today someone pees in unison
with Libby. They exit the stalls at the same time, and
Libby stands face-to-face with Miss Perry, who eyes
Libby's outfit with concern. As Libby washes her
hands, staring into her raw and crusty eyes in the mirror, she suddenly confides to Miss Perry about her
dad.

"Dear, you must go to him now. Give me your
work," Miss Perry says, kindness and duty shining in
her eyes.

"But I don't have any."

Miss Perry looks at her incredulously. "Well, then
you must go now." She ushers Libby to the east wing
coat closet, and by this time Libby is crying, crying
because why hadn't she gone to the prom? So when
Miss Perry accidentally grabs Bilox's coat—long and
black, woven with a touch of cashmere—Libby is
mildly aware it isn't hers, but what difference does it
make at a time like this? Little Bilox, tidy and delicate
as an egg in a nest, is just her size, and she grabs her

token and flees to the subway.

When Bilox comes in the next day wearing her coat, at first Libby thinks he's just being polite by not mentioning the mix-up. But when he leaves for an early appointment, he slips into her velvet-collared wool coat and waves at the room before departing.

It's not that surprising when the sepsis comes. Her dad's body has been invaded at too many points and the armies of antibodies wave a white flag. A ridiculous fever shakes his entire body, a smoldering heat rises from his limbs, and the back of his head, which has been pressed against a pillow for weeks, reveals a strange and snarled hairdo.

Sepsis isn't a bad way to go, the Dumpy Downer tells her. The toxic shock brings on delirium and then coma, after which her dad would float away to a better place, leaving behind his soggy body. Her dad wears a finger cap to monitor his oxygenation, which isn't good, and in his furor he pulls it off and the machine begins a steady ding. Libby places the cap on her own finger and the room is quiet again. Why didn't she fight with that Gestapo nurse yesterday—let him have the damned milkshake! Really, what are they doing here? She doesn't know if she's done right by her father, and she's not sure he's done right by her. He's abandoning ship, and she blames him a little.

Libby walks the twenty blocks from Penn Station
to her apartment just to feel the cold breath of air on
her face. On the way, she stops in a Korean market
and buys a beer and drinks it out of a paper bag. It's
late, but when she gets to her door she finds Hugh
sitting on the stoop, holding a bag of laundry as if it
is a small child. "Maybe you'd like this," he says.

"You can't give me someone else's laundry," she
says, peering into the bag.

"It's been in the lost and found for a year, man."
He looks at her kindly. "You could probably use
some underwear, right?"

"Well, you're sure this is nobody's?" Maybe there
are some towels inside. She needs a clean towel.
Bingo. Inside are four towels, several aprons, knee
socks, a large shapeless sweatshirt with many zippered pockets, and a daisy-printed muumuu.

And so this becomes her routine: in the mornings, Libby pulls on her soft and comfy horror
clothes and puts Bilox's coat over the colorful, shab-
by mess. Then she dashes to the office, sits at Imelda's
desk chewing a nail, waits for Marianne Switzer and
her wire cart, runs the forms in to Bilox, then
Gautreaux, then Sodder, adds her own initials in four
minutes flat, phones Marianne Switzer for a pickup,
dashes down the hall at the sound of the breakfast
cart, shovels a doughnut into her mouth, tosses Miss

Perry a buttered sesame bagel, snatches Bilox's coat from the east wing coat closet, runs for the elevators, thinks bad thoughts all the way to the lobby, flies through the double doors, takes the shuttle across town, hops on the 2 or 3 to Penn Station, scrambles for a ticket, steps onto the Jersey-bound train and falls into a wicked hot sleep.

Libby's mother calls late one night from Chicago, where she's married to a placid radiologist. "Tell me how I can help," she says.

"Do you want to see Dad?"

"Well, no, not that," she says. "I'll come visit you!"

"But I'm never here."

Today Libby's cab sits in a traffic jam en route to the hospital. She pays the driver and gets out and walks, her feet crunching over autumn leaves. Directly across from the hospital is a mini-mall with a deli, a clothes shop and a laundromat. Above the stores are apartments with tiny curtained windows. I should move here, she thinks, digging her hands in Bilox's pockets, which are filled with crumpled bills, sticks of gum, train tickets, ATM receipts.

Her dad's pulled through the sepsis, and he's looking good. In fact, as he becomes sicker he's more alert and the color has returned to his cheeks. Maybe this is some kind of crazy antibiotic flush, a crazy antibiotic buzz.

A boisterous nurse with a smock that pulls across her stomach announces it's time for cognitive tests. "Mr. Meyers, who's the president of the United States?" she asks, checking his intravenous bags. As his body grows waterlogged and inert, they need to check and see that he's still home.

Her dad makes little effort to hide his irritation, but he is more of a charmer than a crab, even in sickness, and finally he smiles wearily. "George Washington," he mouths.

"All right, wise guy," she says. "Let's try movies and entertainment for $500."

He scribbles on his pad, "Frankly my dear I don't give a flying," and then for modesty's sake he's drawn a line.

"Oh!" she hollers. "Mr. Meyers is getting fresh." He offers a half-smile and a silent laugh. He's always been handsome and easy in a reluctant way. Sometimes while he sleeps, the nurses will confide to Libby, "I like your father."

Now as they joke, Libby sees he's already folding in on himself. "Are you in pain?" she whispers. For a moment he's quiet, then shakes his head. He can't name it. They don't have a language for any of this. Libby pats his hand, and his fingers wriggle against the sheet as if movement might carry him somewhere else.

As Libby walks down Eighth Avenue, shivering and drinking a beer out of a paper bag, she bumps into Hugh from the laundromat, who tells her he will personally do her laundry this time. Funny, she asks, but isn't it his personal job to do all the incoming laundry? He tells her he will protect her garments as if her jeans and underwear are the Ten Commandments delivered by God to Moses. She considers letting him wash her horror clothes, but she doesn't trust him. Instead she asks him if he wants to sleep with her. He arrives a bit later, shyly slurping on a chocolate drink, and she greets him at the door wearing the daisy-printed muumuu.

Her law school friends start taking her out for dinners when she arrives back at Penn Station late in the evenings. They eye her speckled clothes, the same mess of a wardrobe she wore through law school, and her headbanded friend Marcy suddenly offers to take her shopping at Loehmann's. "Maybe it's time we found your softer side," she whispers. Libby, tired and drunk, says, "Maybe it's time for one of my friends to do my frigging laundry." But the laundromat can do it for her, Marcy insists. Libby just smiles. They have better jobs than hers, and they insist on tiramisu and picking up the checks. Hang in there, they say nicely.

Her horror friends bring over Chinese food late at night when she's already under the covers in a bathing suit and knee socks, and they spread out all over the floor, eating lo mein with their fingers and discussing tracheotomies, incontinence and hemorrhaging. Sleep, they tell her, we'll lock up when we leave.

Late one evening, Peter the cyclops calls. He's heard about her dad and wants to know if there's anything he can do.

Libby, though wound up and hungry, feels touched. "Come over and do my laundry for me one day."

"No, really?"

"Really."

He hedges and then suggests she take it to the laundromat, where they'll wash, dry and even fold it. Imagine that. "One, two, three," he says.

"I did that and they lost my freaking laundry," she tells him. "It's gone. Vanished!"

"Really?"

"What do you want, Peter?" He's quiet, and it's clear he has nothing to offer. But never mind him; what can she expect from a cyclops? Libby discovers deep in the recesses of her dresser drawer many wearable things—old tank tops and lacy bras with the tags still on. She's running out of clothes again, but there's still something for the morning.

She stuffs her laundry into a backpack, all of it, including the bathing suits and the muumuu, and she takes it to the office, where she packs it up in one of Gautreaux's Seagram's boxes. She addresses the overnight packing slip to the hospital, calls the mail-room for a pickup, and ten minutes later a young man with a wire cart carries the box away.

There is some problem with the elevators. Flashing lights, a bleating noise. Misbuttoning Bilox's coat, Libby weakly considers the stairs, but then she spots the handsome kid who looks like Neil Lubin, who didn't take her to the prom, as he rolls his empty wire cart down the hall. "Is there another way out?" she asks.

"There's always a way out," he says slyly. "Freight elevator."

"Show me," Libby says, hanging onto his sleeve. She's bone-tired and wants a helping hand. Without thinking, she hoists herself onto Imelda's desk and lowers herself into his wire cart. "I have a freaking headache," she explains. He is as kind as he is good-looking. He finds her an aspirin and gives her a paper towel to blow her nose and deposits her outside the service entrance at 44th and Lexington, where a light rain mists their heads.

The next day, the doctors make another attempt to wean her dad from the ventilator, but he struggles for breaths and his eyes dart wildly around the room. Libby stares anxiously at the monitor, which measures his vital signs, as if this will make his lungs work better. He starts mouthing words, and she stands there dumbly, trying to understand until finally she runs into the hall yelling, "He can't do it! He can't!"

Now, exhausted, he sleeps. Libby sits beside him, patting his hand. She wears a cocktail dress, argyle knee socks and the large, shapeless sweatshirt with many zippered pockets. On her dad's nightstand she notices a trick-or-treat bag decorated with goblins and witches. There's a note attached that reads, "Libby, provisions for the long haul. How you doing?" Inside are a combination of sweets and health foods and multivitamins. Libby's eyes tear up, and she is overwhelmed with love for the girlfriends and finds herself wishing they were her friends, wishing her dad could have another chance with one of them if he wanted it.

A friendly nurse brings in the Seagram's box and says, "Do you know what this is?" Before Libby can get out of the chair, the nurse tears off the cover of the box, and together they stare down at the dirty, faintly smelly laundry.

"Mine," Libby says.

Libby grabs quarters from her purse and then

shifts through the trick-or-treat bag, stuffing one of her zippered pockets with a V-8 juice, another with homemade chocolate chip cookies and another with a bottle of multivitamins. The Seagram's box is large and cumbersome, and she weaves unsteadily down the hall until she finds an abandoned wheelchair to place it on. Outside, she rolls the wheelchair across the street to the mini-mall and into the laundromat, past the long line of washers, all of which are in use. The attendant, an elderly man who jingles with coins, looks at her strangely and tells her to come back later. She leaves the Seagram's box and wheels the chair back to the hospital.

Later, when she returns, the air has changed. The darkening sky is a swirl of winter grays, like an old bruise. The same attendant pushes a mop and tells her he's closing in five minutes. She sits on the folding table, as if her unmovable presence will make him soften. The cocktail dress rides up her thighs, exposing the bare skin above her argyle socks. She touches the stubbly hairs.

The attendant sweeps lint into a pile and eyeballs her sitting on the folding table. "I can lock you in, if that's what you want. Do you want me to lock you in?"

"All right." You can never be locked in, only locked out, she reasons. "I'll be very neat," she tells him.

The man finishes sweeping and ties up several garbage bags, turning to her every so often to see if she is still there. Libby tries to smile, but can't quite pull one off. Her body feels leaden and she's struck with the terrible feeling that maybe she, too, is dying. She pats her ears and then feels her neck for enlarged lymph nodes. Reaching into one of the zippered pockets, she pulls out the vitamins and dumps a couple on her tongue. She unzips another pocket and washes them down with a V-8, then unzips another pocket and nibbles on a cookie. She slides her hand under the sweatshirt and does a discreet mini breast exam.

As soon as the man leaves, she separates the whites and darks, gathers her quarters and gets three loads going. She stretches out on the folding table, looks over at the sloshing, soapy water and feels a kind of hope. Please God, she thinks. She doesn't wish for anything in particular, just that things remain as they are a while longer; she simply needs to be suspended in the moment. Time, she believes, is a kind of hope.

The police escort her back to the nurses' station, where the nurses gather around her. There's whispering. The elderly laundry attendant confides, not quietly, that "she looked like a crazy to me." Dumpy Downer impatiently eyes the small crowd and moves toward Libby, touching her elbow.

"I need to speak with you and your father," he says.

"What about my laundry?" Libby asks, looking at the cops, then the nurses and then the mean-spirited laundry attendant. Everyone talks at once, and the cop's radio sputters at noisy intervals. "We know her. It's fine," the friendly nurse says. "There's no need to make a fuss," the boisterous nurse says. Dumpy Downer is now yanking on her arm. Finally, the cops and nurses wind up flirting with each other as Libby is pulled into her dad's room, and the door is closed behind them.

The bottom line, begins Dumpy Downer, is that her dad can't live without a ventilator. His lungs can't do it. They've made every effort. Sad to say, but there's no justification for keeping him in the CCU. He'll have to go upstairs to the ventilator wing. The doctor frowns. He's been through so much. There is another option. They can put him on a morphine drip, make him as comfortable as possible, turn off the ventilator and leave it in God's hands. Libby reels, feeling static travel up her neck and gather in her head. She slumps into a chair. God, she thinks; what does He have to do with it, the slacker. Staring at Dumpy Downer's round, freckled head, she can tell he's not a believer. He believes in medicine, and medicine's failed here. Well, off to the ventilator wing.

"Let's turn off this goddamn thing," her dad writes on his pad. He's sitting up, a picture of health. You flip the switch on invalids; her dad looks as if he could be going to the grocery store. Really, if anyone were to ask, she would have thought that a dying person would be half-gone, unrecognizable, yet her dad is here, terribly present, cocking his head to the side when he hears something dumb. When a vein quivers beneath his eye, he reaches up to touch it.

"Think good and hard," the doctor says, with a finger raised for emphasis. "Good luck, sir."

The doctor shuts the door behind him, and Libby and her dad are left staring at each other. "What an asshole," her dad mouths. She sobs, lowering her head to the bed, and she feels his fingers dance across her hair, light and graceful as Fred Astaire. They are quiet for some time. Finally, she closes her eyes and almost reaches sleep, but at the last second she rushes back from it and lifts her head.

He's laughing without sound. On his pad he's written, "Would you want to go to ventilator wing? What kind of characters are up there?" He's drawn a picture of a skinny little figure covered in a cobweb. She shakes her head. Why make decisions? She wants to hang out. She's got this crazy routine down.

But then he does the unthinkable. He reaches for her hand, tells her how much he loves her, how everything will be okay. He's reaching for movement, to move beyond this moment; his decision's been made. How dare this hospital rush them, how dare they. She simply isn't ready. She heads for the door, throws it open and yells into the quiet, pale hallway, "DO NOT RUSH US!"

The nurses' station is unoccupied, but on a wheel-chair by the door is the Seagram's box filled with clean, folded laundry. She touches it, and it's still warm.

BEAUTIFUL GIRLS

FOR DAYS NOW SOMETHING HAD REEKED IN THE basement. None of us went down there, no laundry had been done and our mother had to hand-wash her stuff in the sink. She now stood in the kitchen in her pantyhose and mink, cursing, as she waved the blow drier over her fancy black bra while Franz waited for her in the living room.

"Find that stink!" she yelled suddenly, chasing my little sisters around the dining room table. "Or I'll throw all of you out."

"Good!" Daffodil yelled. She was nine. "I'll go live at Shoshanna's. They don't have to eat roast beef every single night!"

"Shoshanna's, my ass. Here, you want some variety? How about an eyeround?" Mom opened the refrigerator and tossed a package of beef that landed next to Daffodil's foot.

Feeling hungry, I picked up the piece of meat. "Hey Mom, 300 degrees for an hour?" I asked.

"350. 45 minutes."

"We should hire someone to go down the cellar and find the stink," Dorrie shrieked. "Like the boy who cleaned the rain gutters." Dorrie was eleven and geeky with long, jagged teeth that didn't fit right in her mouth. She wasn't pretty like me or Daffodil. She looked more like our mother, big-toothed and sulky. Both my sisters, though, looked Italian while I looked more French, I thought. "We could hire someone," Dorrie said again.

"Do you think I'm made of money, Miss Priss?"

"Then send Franz," I offered.

Mom's faced flushed and her hands flew up to her hair. "We are not asking Franz because you three will take your little behinds down there, find the stink and get rid of it. Do you hear me, Dani?" She wasn't fooling me; she believed Franz was too good for our stink.

Mom had met Franz through the freezer plan. Once a month he would come with his list and Mom would check off what we needed—two packets of pork chops, a crown roast, a London broil—and the frozen hunks of meat would arrive in individual frosty plastic pouches, which my sisters and I would unload into the gigantic freezer in the basement.

Now with the stink, we unloaded right into the refrigerator.

As Mom glared at us, a skinny, sagging breast slipped out of her mink coat and gazed at us.

"Your tit, Mom," I said. Luckily, I hadn't inherited that gene; mine were full and firm, perfect handfuls. But I was seventeen.

Inggy stared into the mud, smiling, and I felt drunk all over, even my fingers felt stupid. The crème de menthe and Quaalude sloshed in my stomach as the band played the theme song to "Hawaii Five-O," and we spun on the sidelines with our shakers high in the air. The noise swelled in my bones and Inggy's bones and everyone's bones—as if all bones were connected; I could tell Inggy felt it too. She closed her eyes and looked to the sky as if she were praying.

Ingrid Oberlander, my best friend, was the color of milk with shiny blonde hair hanging down to her butt. At 5'11", she was the boniest and most beautiful person I knew. She wanted to be a psychoanalyst and carried around a bent-up copy of *The Portable Jung* and gave me personality tests. We found out that I was ENFP, meaning I was lively, deeply psychic, prone to ulcers, a bit wishy-washy and a softy at heart.

Inggy swooped down and hugged me tightly. "My friend," she said.

"No, my friend," I said.

When the music stopped, Lauralynn Figuero, captain of our lame squad, shouted "Hey! You!" and we got into a line for attitude time.

"Hey you," we sang, pointing our fingers at the school across the field and shaking our hips.

"Hey you, sitting over there
you'd better get your ass right out of that chair,
because I'm telling you once
and you better beware
we're gonna fuck you right on up,
WE'RE-GONNA-FUCK-YOU-RIGHT-ON-UP,
we'regonnafuckyourightonup."

We danced, lifting our skirts and shaking our asses at the band as we shouted the chorus once again. No one paid attention to us, and we started knocking into each other, moving in cranky, drunken circles. The sky looked like it was ready to break open.

Ben sat on the bench with ice on his leg, scanning the crowd as he chewed on a pretzel. He was a middle linebacker and one of my favorite people. Once he was my boyfriend for ten days until all the fun went out of it. Pamela Zlotkin, who stood in the bleachers with the drill team, waved to him and mouthed his name. Rumor was her parents spent a thousand dollars to send her to modeling school. She was no better-looking now; she was still an attractive girl in a horsey kind of way, and like a caribou she migrated in a herd to the water fountain, cafeteria line, wall mirror outside of the gym. She wasn't a friend of mine but she was all right, I supposed.

The rain started lightly. I felt it on the top of my head and the rim of my ears. Some kids in the band opened umbrellas. My muscles were tight and cold, and I kicked my leg up alongside my body to stretch it out. I did a sloppy back handspring and muddied my hands. I was restless and numb at the same time, and I let the rain soak me. From where I stood I counted three guys in the bleachers I'd slept with, another leaning on the fence. Then I counted Ben sitting on the sidelines and even Kipper Coleman, the waterboy, because he was kind of cute in a goofy way. I moved in half a circle and counted two more guys on the field and the assistant to the assistant coach, who didn't really count because I only gave him a blow job. Then I lost count. I rubbed on cherry lip gloss, blinking into the rain. I'd never been in love. I wondered about love and was there a right love and a wrong love—was getting naked with a cute boy and watching his eyes soften and feeling my heart pound high in my chest—was that a little like the real thing?

Yesterday, with one hand, Ben had swept his bed clean of socks and sweats and CDs. I stood naked beside him looking down at my breasts, feeling good.

The small of his back was pimply; I touched him
there as I had many times, and then we snuggled on
the same warm and funky-smelling pillow, smoking
what was left of a joint. It didn't make me high, but
it made me laugh inside my head for about thirty seconds. Ben's mom, Connie, was coming home soon,
and together the three of us would eat spaghetti and
meatballs. The Stones sang in the background.

I placed my palm over Ben's heart and felt it beat-
ing there, strong and quick, rising up to meet my
hand. A boy's heart, I thought. The dark blue light of
dusk filled the room. I kissed his collarbone, running
my fingers over his chest until he leaned down and
took my face between his hands. He looked at me
hard, not like he thought I was pretty, but as if he
were memorizing me. I let him look at me like that
until I started to feel ugly. "Hey," I said, squirming.

He blinked, smiled, then kissed my forehead, my
nose, my cheeks, my lips. "I like you, Dani," he whispered.

"I know," I said.

After the football game, Inggy and I walked the
few blocks to my house, where we napped in my twin
bed, sleeping head to feet. Later as we woke, untwist-
ing ourselves from the sheets, we were crabby and
raccoon-eyed with heads of tangled hair. I poked at
mine with a comb, and Inggy tied hers back with a

sock while Daffodil whined at my door to please let her in. She was extra-in-love with the two of us ever since the senior class had chosen Inggy and me as two of five nominees for the Miss Merry Christmas Contest. "Don't be too impressed, Daff, we're still the same cruddy girls," Inggy said through the door.

"It's hardly the big time," I added.

Inggy kept a stash of clothes in one of my drawers, since she could never go home high or drunk and would sleep over at my place instead. We both changed into jeans, debating our evening options. Outside, it was dark and chilly, and my mom and Franz were out on the town.

In the kitchen, Dorrie and Daffodil burned popcorn while they waited for George, their dad, to pick them up. He showed up pretty regularly and took them bowling, or to the batting cage or an arcade on the Jersey shore. He often asked if I wanted to come along. But I didn't like him. "You're a pretty thing," he'd once said, letting his eyes wander all over me. Number one, I didn't need him telling me I was pretty; number two, he was about forty years old; and numbers three, four and five, Dorrie and Daffodil were my sisters, he was their father, and he'd lived with us when I was a little kid.

My own father had pulled a Houdini a long time ago. I only knew him by the check that was supposed to come at the beginning of each month but didn't always.

He had just erased me, I guessed, pretended I hadn't happened. But still, did he ever wonder how I was turning out? It was clear to me how he'd turned out.

Inggy and I grabbed handfuls of burnt popcorn for the road, said goodbye to my sisters, and set out for a keg party.

As the beer ran out and the party broke up, most everyone headed for the front lawn. A few bodies were strewn throughout the hallway and draped across assorted chairs. Our host—this kid John—whose parents, I'd heard, were in Atlantic City for the weekend, was asleep on the recliner. I sat at the kitchen table and peered into the living room at Inggy and Kevin McSweeney, who sat on a big lumpy couch, quietly holding hands.

Moments later, Inggy joined me, flush-faced and nervously fingering the buttons of her sweater. "I'm sure Kevin's an INFJ."

"How do you know so much? Telepathy?"

"We talked, nosey."

I sucked up beer through a straw, watching as Pamela Zlotkin stood on the curb and loudly offered rides home in her Nissan. "Aren't you starving?" I asked.

"Completely and absolutely." In this John kid's refrigerator, his parents had left him—we counted—twenty hamburger patties. We didn't think he'd mind, so I fried us up a couple of his hamburgers while Inggy explained to me how two similar personality types are naturally drawn to each other while the idea of opposites, who supposedly attract, is highly questionable and overrated. "Jung got it wrong," she says. "Don't you think?"

I nodded. My opposite would be a quiet, territorial, practical, logical, facts-first decision-maker. I didn't know boys like that and hoped I never would. But the way I thought about the boys I liked best was different; I thought about their contradictions—how they were soft yet fierce, happy but all chewed up on the inside.

"Do you think Kevin's cute, Dani?" Inggy asked, biting into her burger.

"Kind of." She gazed at me mildly. Kevin had a long hangdog face and wide eyes that drooped in their sockets, and while he played a mean game of basketball, he had a bad slouch off the court.

"I do," she said.

I reached across the table and rubbed her hand, feeling the delicate bones and the small swell of blue veins and wondered what it meant to be Inggy inside that long stretch of white skin. As pretty as she was she'd only been kissed once in her seventeen years. "He's got a certain something," I said. From the window, I watched Ben climb into the front seat of Pamela Zlotkin's Nissan.

When my sisters and I ran out of clean underwear, Dorrie had to resume laundry duty despite the
stink. She'd hold her nose, run down the cellar stairs,
get a load going and run back up, looking like she
might blow chunks. No one but Dorrie had set foot
down there. Mom fought with us daily, yelling, yanking on our skinny arms, but no one was budging.

Mom, who was now all dressed up, wearing her
mink and Chanel No. 5, gathered us in the den one
night while Franz waited for her in the living room. A
full moon shone through the window behind her.
"Cook up a steak and potatoes for supper, ladies,"
she told us, and then lowering her voice added, "And
when I come home, I want the stink gone. I want it
out of our lives."

"We're beautiful girls!" Daffodil said, linking arms
with me. "You can't expect us to go down there!"

This kind of talk really ticked Mom off, and she
tilted her head to the side and gave Daffodil a cockeyed smile. "God is punishing us with the stink
because you're conceited and stuck-up."

"I *am* stuck-up," Daffodil agreed, and a tiny sigh
escaped through her lips.

"It's very rude," Mom snapped.

"She is rude," I agreed.

"You're stuck-up, too," Mom said.

"I'm really not," I said.

"I guess I am, too," Dorrie said.

"You are not stuck-up," Mom said, but she regarded Dorrie with the same disappointment.

"Ask Franz to find the stink," Daffodil said finally. "That's what boyfriends are for."

Mom lifted her hand. "I'm leaving. Do what I asked." And she turned on her three-inch heels and left us for the evening.

"I'm starvin' Marvin," Daffodil said. I popped the steak in the broiler while the girls set the table. Then Dorrie and I took turns standing on the stepstool and mashing the potatoes while Daffodil roused us with a Pop Warner cheer, ending with a crash to the linoleum in a split. The meat was rare the way we liked it, and I cut thick slabs. My sisters sat in their seats, forks poised in the air, ketchup globs dainty and jewel-like on their plates.

I got thrown out of Anthropology because I'd accidentally dropped my bracelet onto the second-story ledge outside the window. In the girls' room, I climbed out on the ledge and walked past Humanities and U.S. History and made my way back to Pickett's class where my bracelet lay. Pickett, who must have been eighty, opened the window and when I tried to tell her I was fine, she reached for me with her age-spotted hands and hauled me in. As I sat in the principal's office, I checked my biology homework and read a chapter of *Daisy Miller*.

I got to Advanced Biology late but I still had my pick of a frog or a clam. I wasn't in the mood for an invertebrate so I took the frog, went back to my station and sliced it open, correctly labeling the digestive and reproductive systems. I saw a fly in the stomach, small and perfect, not yet digested, its wings close to its body as if at rest.

After school, Inggy and Kevin lingered in front of her locker, talking. She seemed to be on the brink of love, wavering there, unsteady. I waved goodbye, feeling sort of itchy and jealous and not knowing what to do with myself. I thought about stopping by the Exxon station and visiting Colin who I fooled around with now and then.

Ben's sweatshirt was spotted with big raindrops and his workboots were untied as he plodded up to me. He gave me a slow smile as he leaned against a locker. "Stoner," I said, looking into his bloodshot eyes.

"Slob," he said, looking into my locker at the mess of books, crumpled papers, candy wrappers and medicated acne pads.

"Want to go to your house?" I brushed the knots out of my hair.

He shook his head. "You toy with me."

"Ha!" I yelled, but when I turned to him he looked disgusted and far away. *You toy with me.* The words were strange and flat in the air above us. "That's a rotten thing to say," I finally said. "Are you mad at me?"

He shook his head and slid down the locker to the floor, rubbing his temples. I stared at his big feet. "I used to wait, thinking you'd want to be my girl-friend again, but you don't and now I don't want you to be—so what are we doing here?" He placed his hands out in front of him, and I looked at the space between them, a space I could slide right into if I wanted to. His hands fell to his lap, and I squatted down next to him and thought about touching him.

"So, okay, we're not going to be boyfriend and girlfriend," I said quietly.

"We're just going to be friends." We sat in the hallway as other kids filtered by, their voices echoing down the hall. In the silence, Ben was telling me we wouldn't get naked anymore, we wouldn't talk on the phone at midnight, we wouldn't hang out at his house, we wouldn't hang out together with Connie. He was also telling me about Pamela Zlotkin. He was telling me many things I didn't want to hear.

It'd been raining for days, and the wintry sky hung low over the town. I rode my bike down Main Street, empty and slick with puddles, and stared at the posters of five smiling girls in the store windows. There we were—me, Inggy, Pamela Zlotkin and two

other girls—Miss Merry Christmas nominees—dis-
played next to shoes, pizza pies, postage stamps and
interest rates, waiting for the town to crown a winner.
I parked under a street lamp and stared and stared,
secretly feeling the thrill of good luck and good
genes. It was a decent picture of me, not like I must
have looked now—a girl in the rain with her hair
plastered to her head.

Even though it embarrassed me to admit it, I really really wanted to win. I wanted to see what winning
might do for me. But I knew Inggy would win; she
seemed destined. At the moment the school photog-
rapher had snapped her picture, the wind swept a
long strand of white hair clear over her head and she
hollered with glee. I remembered thinking this was
what Daisy Miller must have looked like before the
malaria. Inggy was the most beautiful girl on the
poster, although there was more to it than that. On
that windy November day she was there in her photo,
fully herself.

I let myself in the side door where Connie stood
at the stove making a big pot of chicken soup. "Hey,
you," she said. "Rice or egg noodles?"

"Rice." Ben and Pamela Zlotkin had gone to the
movies. The news spread fast today, reaching my ears
in Advanced Biology as I classified algae under the
microscope.

Connie threw me a dish towel, and I patted my wet head.

"I think Ben really likes this Pam Zlotkin girl," I said. I thought I wanted to talk about this, to hear words instead of my own rattling thoughts.

Connie smiled. "You okay, Dani?"

"Sure," I lied. Something felt lost, something I didn't think I wanted. Connie put a bowl of soup in front of me and handed me a spoon. I felt flushed and confused, the heat of soup and memories welling up inside of me. "Do you think I broke his heart, Connie?" Lately I'd been counting my favorite people: Inggy, Ben, Connie. I would say their names to myself, carrying them with me like essential items in my pocketbook—lip gloss, money, keys. I hoped I hadn't broken him, yet part of me hoped I had.

Connie skimmed the fat off the top of the pot, dropping the grease into a measuring cup. She smiled into the soup. "You two will always be friends, don't you think?"

I nodded weakly, but I wanted to know about the state of his heart. I wanted to know about the state of mine. "If Pam Zlotkin becomes his girlfriend, how will I ever come over here?" I asked.

"You better come over, Dani." I'd once run mayonnaise through Connie's hair to give it some shine and she wound up with greasy hair for a week, but she was so cool about it. She wrapped a bandanna around her head and that was that. I couldn't imagine not having her as my friend, not spending time in this house. Sometimes on a Saturday night Ben and I would pull out the sleeping bags and watch late movies. We'd fool around and fall asleep with popcorn still in our teeth. When we woke up, Connie would make French toast, and wrapped in sweaters we'd eat on the porch with the morning light washing over us.

I wondered how much Connie knew about me and Ben, though her knowing everything might have changed things between us. I wanted to tell her this: As my friend, Ben had a life and there were other things in his line of vision. But as his girlfriend, his life shrunk and I was the only thing playing on his screen. Seeing Ben at the end of the day waiting by my locker became as ordinary and predictable as rolling out of bed in the morning. I just thought I wanted *more*. I didn't know what, but was pretty sure I'd know if I found it, or if it found me.

Connie came up behind me and kissed me lightly on top of my wet head.

I snuggled with Daffodil on the couch in the den while Mom and Franz fought in the living room. They'd been having spats all week, and they'd stopped smiling at each other and started rolling their eyes when they thought the other wasn't looking. "Trouble," Dorrie said, from the other end of the couch, where she chewed on a strand of hair.

Daffodil wore a sequined purple bodysuit, and her dark, shiny hair was pulled into a ponytail. Violet eye shadow sparkled above her long lashes. "What's this?" I said, wiping her face clean with the bottom of my T-shirt.

"Get off," she yelled.

"You want to turn into a slut?"

"No," she yelled.

"Then clean up your act."

She already had boys calling the house, but it wasn't anything really. She'd say, "You're a faggot." Then he'd say, "No, you are." "No, you." "You." "You."—like that until one of them would get tired and say, "See you tomorrow." Now she rubbed up against me. She wanted to be me; she would tell me this. "You're going to be Miss Merry Christmas," she whispered.

"Yeah, maybe."

"You're the prettiest," she said. Her teeth were tiny and white, her eyes all dark pupils. Her head lay in the crook of my arm, and she motioned for me to bring my ear close. I leaned down and she told me how she and some of her older friends, girls in the fourth and fifth grades, had gone to every store on Main Street and voted for me, filling out a white slip and dropping it into the box beneath our pictures. "I disguised my handwriting," she whispered. "Don't worry."

After my sisters and I had pigged out on pot roast and gravy, I started wondering if Ben might call me. I lay on the couch, shaving my legs and dipping the razor into a Dixie cup filled with soapy, hairy water. Dorrie and Daffodil lay on their backs on the carpet, painting their fingernails red. After a bitter fight, Mom and Franz were out to dinner. The phone was silent.

Inggy walked through the front door. "Hey, Dan," she yelled, coming into the den and spreading college catalogs all around the coffee table. We had to start thinking of these things, she told me. Look at this, check this out—she spoke a mile a minute. "This one has environmental science." There was a picture of a weenie kid standing in a sludgy bog, holding a beaker. "What kind of science do you like best?" she asked me. I shrugged, dropping the razor into the Dixie cup.

"Dorrie," I said, "go get me some socks, will you?"

"Get your own," she said, blowing on a nail. "I'm not going down there."

"We've got a stink," Daffodil told Inggy. Inggy opened the cellar door and gagged. "Come away from there," Daffodil said, taking her hand.

"Are you guys waiting until the whole house is a giant stink bomb? Let's see what it is, Dani."

"Inggy, *sit down*," I said, getting pissed off. She came over here, waving catalogs, telling me to be some scientist, telling me what to do about the stink. I stared into that sludgy-brown bog, wishing she could somehow fall into it.

"Come on, lazy," she said, giving me a tug.

"Leave it alone, Inggy," I said, quietly. Daffodil and Dorrie looked at me, their red nails flashing brightly. Inggy looked at me for a second, then started down the cellar stairs. I hated her then; for a few burning seconds I loathed my friend, who was beautiful and faultless and braving the stinking basement. I leapt off the couch and grabbed one of her long arms and easily yanked her up the steps. "I'll see you later," I said, pushing the catalogs into her arms.

"Dani!" Inggy cried. "Are you insane?"

"Out," I whispered.

"No!" Inggy said. Daffodil and Dorrie crept up beside me and eyed Inggy. We stood there tensely, and I finally shoved Inggy toward the front door, and Dorrie and Daffodil jumped in, poking and jabbing. We spun big skinny Inggy in a circle, her catalogs falling out of her arms. We knocked into a wall, jiggling a picture. "Our stink," I cried, "is none of your business."

"You big snoop," Daffodil hollered, giving her a

kick in the shin.

"Who do you think you are?" Dorrie shouted, pulling a wad of that white hair. We got Inggy to the front door and pushed her onto the stoop. I locked the door behind her, feeling lost and sick. My best friend in the world. So cocky, so sure of herself. I wouldn't be Miss Merry Christmas, she would.

She rang the doorbell. Inggy never rang the bell, she always walked right in.

"What?" I said, opening the door a crack.

"Dani," she said with tears in her eyes.

Daffodil squeezed in next to me and gave Inggy the evil eye. "Don't," I said, clasping Daffodil's small head and nudging her away. "Inggy," I said, "I'll call you later."

We trooped back into the den and sat on the couch, not saying anything. I knew what we had to do. We had to take some action. It was time. The stench was dizzying, and my sisters clutched my arms as we made our way downstairs. Daffodil went straight to the clothesline in the back of the cellar, pinched shut her nose with a clothespin and then stood in the corner with her eyes tightly closed, her glittery bodysuit and matching socks shimmering in the low light.

Dorrie started to sniff while I stood on a bucket and opened all the windows the best I could. Dorrie pointed under the freezer. Holding my nose, I kneeled.

Something was wedged underneath. I used the mop handle and worked out a putrid, decaying pork chop with a swarm of wriggling maggots inside. Daffodil came running over, and both my sisters looked up at me with big eyes. "Gross," Dorrie whispered.

"How did the bugs get inside, Dani?" Daffodil asked.

I said a leftover summer fly must've thought the stinking pork chop was a great place to lay eggs. "Which one of you dopes dropped the chop?" They each pointed a mean little finger at the other. I went for the shovel, Daffodil propped the front door open, and Dorrie dragged a garbage can to the curb. I scooped up the rotting chop and sailed up the stairs and through the front door, stopping short on the lawn. Garbage pick-up wasn't for three more days. The stink would still be with us.

"Let's bury it," I said.

We stood in the backyard under a dark moon and a web of stringy clouds, digging a hole. "Give me an 'S,'" Daffodil shouted. "Give me a 'T,' give me an 'I-N-K.'" Shivering, Dorrie and I took turns working the shovel into the hard ground, and when we got a semi-deep cockeyed hole I kicked in the chop and covered it with dirt. We stomped on the hole, dancing it smooth with our feet.

"The stink is out of our lives!" I yelled.

"Victory cheer!" Dorrie shouted.

"Oooolala we kicked some ass
Oooolala we showed some sass
Oooolala we had some fun
Oooolala of course we won!"

We did the chicken walk across the hole, flapping our elbows and wobbling our knees. We buzzed around each other and gave high fives and whooped it up. A few of our neighbors' porch lights went on, and we whooped it up some more. We did spring rolls in front of the bushes and flying wontons along the weedy fence. Daffodil started turning cartwheels, one after the other, and Dorrie and I joined in, the three of us whirling crazy under the night sky. Then I did a vault over a garbage can, my hands pushing off the lid and my legs spread wide, as I shot through the cold air and landed with a one-two hop right in front of my sisters. Their eyes were hugely dark and alive, their hair popping out of the elastics, their breath coming out in frosty little clouds.

Daffodil grabbed me tightly and covered me with frantic kisses. Dorrie's eyes traveled carefully from me to Daffodil, from me to Daffodil, and watching her watch us, I understood how things were for Dorrie. My heart caught and I turned away. As we ran to the back door, I reached for Dorrie, but she dipped under my arm and sprang up the steps.

Inggy and I sat on the bed of the float sharing a
bag of corn chips and staring at her one-hundred-
dollar bill. It was crisp and new and made a snapping
noise when the wind gathered beneath us. "I wish
we'd both won," she said. I nodded halfheartedly.
She folded the bill in half, hiked up her cape, and
pocketed it.

Today Inggy wore a little pearly eye shadow and
some lipstick, and the rhinestone tiara sparkled on
her head. The red velvet cape was too short on her
and her jeans and sneakers stuck out the bottom.
Pamela Zlotkin and the other girls and I wore white
velvet capes. I wore my hair up and thought I looked
particularly French.

A folding chair was perched atop the specially
made staircase sitting in the middle of the float.
"Come," I said, climbing the staircase because I
wanted to try out the chair and see the view. The day
was cold, crisp and gray. Behind us were our school's
marching band, flag twirlers, a float with gift-
wrapped people standing around a Christmas tree,
another float with assorted elves. "Inggy," I whispered, "What's going to happen to us?"

"Good things, good things," she said, checking
out Main Street. There were honks and toots and
mini drum rolls as the band warmed up. A baton shot
through the air and plummeted into a twirler's hand.

"Places, girls," a fat man from the Chamber of

Commerce said to us, and I slowly climbed down and took my place on the right rear corner of the float. Next to me were Styrofoam stars attached to broom handles.

We crept along to the tune of "We Wish You a Merry Christmas" as people on the sidewalks waved to us. Inggy's parents, the very tall and brightly blond Oberlanders, snapped pictures and galloped along-side us for a block. "Inggy! Dani!" they called. "Over here, love. Big, big smile." Inggy sat on the folding chair, flushed yet pleased, beaming her big, big smile down on her mom and dad.

Mom and Franz had decided to call it quits, and she'd taken to wearing dark glasses as if someone had died. She demanded super quiet. Even walking around in our socks and opening the refrigerator door would make her scream and send us scattering to far corners of the house. This morning I'd left her on the couch with her diet soda, Motrin, box of tissues, can of mixed nuts, and the *TV Guide*, and I knew she'd still be on the couch when I got home, that she might be there for a long time. I hoped she'd find a new boyfriend, I hoped she'd soon put on her three-inch heels again and leave us in peace. But why couldn't she have dragged her butt off the couch and brought the Instamatic and been here today? Even if it was me up there on the folding chair with the crown on my head, I knew she'd still be horizontal under the afghan in her dark glasses.

There was nothing to do but wave my arm. My sisters were boycotting the parade, at least that was what they said for the hundredth time when I left them this morning, slurping up Fruit Loops and glued to cartoons. The week before when they found out I hadn't won they both cried, but it was Daffodil who sobbed, huge tears running down her blotchy face, her whole body heaving. Maybe she had wanted me to pave the way for her. "You like Inggy, right?" I'd said, holding her hand.

"Not anymore."

"But I get to ride on the float, too."

"So what?" she sobbed.

I hoped they'd change their minds, and I kept a lookout for their pompomed hats as we rolled along. There was so much noise—"Deck the Halls," the clapping and cheering, Santa and his ho ho ho's. Kevin McSweeney leapt out of the crowd and ran alongside us, gaping up at Inggy. I looked for Ben but didn't see him until we passed the hardware store, where he and a couple of his friends were sitting on bags of fertilizer. We both waved, but I couldn't tell if we were waving to each other. "Ben," I heard myself whisper. "Ben." What if he'd been meant for me and me for him?

Up ahead on the sidewalk Connie waved to Pamela Zlotkin, who stood on the front of our float, and I wondered if they liked each other. I wondered if Pamela had sat in Connie's warm kitchen on the chair with the blue polka-dotted cushion next to the radiator, the chair I always sat in. Connie saw me and blew a kiss. I blew one back and turned and stared in her direction long after we passed.

Then I saw my sisters, hiding behind a mailbox in front of the savings and loan and watching for me. As the float glided toward them, they pushed their way into the street and stood there wide-eyed while I waved like mad. "That's my sister!" Daffodil shouted, pointing at me. Both Dorrie and Daffodil looked as if they were waiting for something to happen, and I too almost expected something to happen then, but the float coasted on indifferently like a cloud through the sky, and I lost them in the crowd.

The air was still and calm and cold. I'd heard it would snow later tonight, the first snow of the year. It was only supposed to be a light dusting, but I hoped it would be enough to cover the town in a clean sheet of white.

All of a sudden we stopped short. I stumbled, nearly stepping on Inggy's tiara, which landed by my feet. It was hard to see what was happening so I climbed up the little staircase to Inggy, carrying her crown, and saw that up ahead a car had rear-ended a police cruiser at the intersection of Maple and Main, causing everything to come to a stop. Inggy inched over and I shared the folding chair with her. "You're not crying, Dani, are you?" she said.

"I'm not crying," I said. She slung an arm over my shoulder and pulled the bag of corn chips from under her cape. That's all I wanted then, to sit beside Inggy, eating corn chips and watching the standstill up ahead.

In front of us, the ladies' auxiliary put down their banner and lit cigarettes. Pamela Zlotkin still stood on her corner of the float, waving to a crowd that wasn't paying attention while the two other girls hunched together in their billowy white velvet capes and seemed to be reading each other's palms. I wondered what they saw there.

EDEN

LET'S CALL OUR COUPLE ADAM AND EVE SINCE THEY'LL be visiting paradise. Both Adam and Eve are accompanying their mothers on a cruise from Africa to India and the islands in between. Four hundred passengers board the ship in Kenya. Adam and Eve haven't met yet, and they don't notice each other as they roll their suitcases along the Marina Deck in search of the elevators to their respective cabins, which they'll share with their respective mothers. Soon—not today—they'll meet. They'll learn they both live on the East Coast; that they both have high metabolisms; that they're both easily exasperated by their mothers; that they're both flirty yet wary.

Adam is a hippie who teaches junior high and has two children by two different women and lives in the

Pine Barrens of New Jersey, where he has an out-
house and fruit trees. He's a vegetarian. He's also
boyish and compact and a tad persnickety.

Eve is a dark-eyed, woolly-haired carnivore who
likes to chomp on the turkey leg on Thanksgiving.
She's a dreamy, occasionally crabby person. She's a
clothes buyer for Lord & Taylor and lives in New York
City and has been on many bad blind dates this year.

On day two of the trip Adam and Eve unofficial-
ly meet in Zanzibar. It's sunrise and they're the only
two on the deck as the ship heads for the lush palm
tree-covered island. Wooden dhows dip and sway in
the pulse of the water. There's a heavy scent of cloves.
Adam and Eve sniff the air and give each other the
once-over.

They officially meet on the island of Mayotte,
where they swim with turtles and drip dry under the
ylang-ylang trees. Adam plucks a flower, crushes it,
and puts his fragrant fingers beneath Eve's nose.
"Smell this," he says. It's the most gorgeous scent
that's ever filled her nose, and she almost drops to her
knees in the sand. She takes this as a sign from
God—a sign of what she isn't quite sure.

It isn't long before Adam and Eve are sneaking
around the ship in the wee hours. She sticks her
tongue in his ear in the library; he feels her up in the
engine room; they get half-naked on the Lido Deck

after midnight, where the warm wind makes them shiver. Adam has dark, wet eyes and a tidy ponytail. He has a way of tilting his head and gazing at her full strength as if he can see her down to her bones. "Your hair," he murmurs, "is crazy fantastic." And it is! In New York her hair is all wrong, her curls often a fuzzy, startled nest. But here on the Indian Ocean she has loose, snaky tendrils—a voluptuous seaweed head.

Eve gallops along the deck at sunset, past all the retirees out for a stroll. The sky is scorched with color. Love, love, love, she whispers out to sea. Oh, *love*, she thinks mistily—I can't wait to get to know this Adam guy.

But she knows this isn't love, only her desire to love and be loved in return. The trouble is she's gone too long without feeling special. She's gone too long without gazing into the eyes of someone dear. She's been out with one too many drips. She's had a major drought and is ready for a little drizzle.

During their days at sea Adam and Eve loll in the saltwater pool, mute as driftwood. The sun beats down on Eve's head, and she realizes she hasn't been thinking complete thoughts. She looks south and thinks there's only water between us and Antarctica. There: a complete thought. Everything on this journey is about pleasure. The pleasure of sunshine, powdery white sand, the blue-green sea; the pleasure of hands and hair and bellies. Just last week she was plowing through Midtown, jaywalking, dodging taxis and buses—tense as a skyscraper, a 5'2" nerve ending. Here her limbs are splayed and bare, idle as a jellyfish.

There is the problem of ditching their moms. Adam and Eve gobble through their respective dinners and then sit with their mothers in the Diamond Lady Lounge for the tango show or an evening with the Sea Dynasty singers and dancers. Later when their moms have gone to bed, they meet up at the Water Hole or the Tip Top Bar for cigars under the stars. Adam hugs Eve tightly, cigar smoke twisting above their heads. She swoons. "Adam," she whispers.

"Eve," he whispers back.

Not that it's perfect, though it almost is. He rubs her back and pulls the label out of her tank top. "What is this? Acrylic?" he asks.

"It's microfiber. Like it?"

"I like natural fibers," he says.

When the sky begins to lighten they sneak back to their respective cabins, waking their respective moms, who eye their respective clocks.

Adam phones Eve at eight-thirty one morning. "Come quick," he says. His mom is going to the beauty salon in the bowels of the ship. "How long does a pedicure take?" he asks. Eve throws on a bikini and shorts and grabs her key.

"I thought we were going to the champagne

breakfast," her mom says, squeezing into a girdle. She squats, hoists, wriggles it up. "You'd rather run all over God's creation with that hippie than spend time with me."

Of course I would, Eve thinks. *Oh, Mom.* Eve wants to be loved deeply, tragically, completely. It shames her, but after all these years she still hopes for the fairy tale. She wants to believe there's a prince of a guy, tucked into her future, who will one day unfurl like a robust, exotic bloom in the weedy patch of her life. That's the way it is with Eve—the way it has been since she can remember. "Oh Mom," she says. "I'll meet you there. Save me a chocolate croissant."

Eve flies down two flights to the Laguna Deck and down the skinny corridor to where Adam is putting the "Do Not Disturb" sign on his door. They tumble onto his little twin bed, yanking off clothes and pulling each other close, quick and naughty as if they're teenagers. "Alone at last," Eve cries. And just when they are naked and tangled the key turns in the lock.

"I forgot to take my multivitamin!" Adam's mother cries, as Adam and Eve grab the covers. Adam's mom snatches the bottle off the dresser and shakes one out. "Really Adam, if you want me to shoo, just tell me to shoo. I'm only paying for this trip." After she leaves they huddle under the covers, ashamed, quietly playing footsie. Next to the bed is a pair of Adam's mom's felt slippers with little button eyes, watching them.

All Eve wants is to have sex in private. She wants to lie down between sheets next to Adam. She wants to rest her head on his chest, pretending he is hers, even though he is not and she doesn't know him well enough to know if she would want him to be. But still…She wants to see how it might feel, how it might be. This fling has the whiff of something delirious— Vick's VapoRub, gasoline.

They do what they can. On Nosy Komba, Madagascar, she gives him a hand job on a tree-topped hill while golden-eyed lemurs swing from the branches above them. On Nosy Be, they hump behind a mud hut.

In the Seychelles they attempt underwater inter-course. They swim away from the watchful eyes of the other passengers, toward the reef where they pull off their bathing suits and tread water. But they slide off each other and sink, and Eve's bikini bottom almost floats away. The trouble is Adam's too soft, the watery angles are wrong, and they get nosefuls of the salty sea. Finally, they give up. Beneath them the water is clear as light, and there's a tremulous city of slippery neon fish, downy rocks, and fallopian plant life. They stare down at their reedy, naked legs—pale sea anemones—pumping in the current. Their pubic hair is pulsing and alive. What perfect sea creatures they've become!

At $1.75 per minute, Eve e-mails her friends back home. In the subject section she writes, *I think I've found the one!* She tells her friends all about Adam, his lovely yin-yang tattoo. She complains about the lack of privacy, the lack of sexual opportunity, their mothers.

Her mystically inclined friend Miranda e-mails back. "Hip hip hooray! And New Jersey! He's practically right around the corner. But, honey, how long have you known this guy? A week? Some Native Americans believe the first time with a new partner should take place in the woman's bed, otherwise little pieces of her spirit are lost, and as far I know they're not recoverable. This is the way it is with women, unfortunately. I'm only mentioning this because you're so far from home. Do you really want to lose a piece of yourself on the Indian Ocean? If he's as delicious as you say, wait. Save intercourse for America— on the Upper West Side in your Murphy bed."

Eve spends the next five minutes in a gloomy funk because Miranda—wise, dear Miranda—is often right about many things. This could be a potentially irksome quality, but Miranda is a radiant being, charming and self-deprecating, and she pulls off righteousness without too many snags.

Eve hasn't always had first-time sex in her own bed and wonders if she's had some soul leakage in the San Fernando Valley, the East Village, Weehawken.

She also wonders if soul leakage could be related to the melancholy that sometimes swells inside her like music.

She shoots back an e-mail. "Thanks for the spirit tip. I'll try to wait, but I'm in paradise…"

She presses Send, and exits the cave-like e-mail center and hangs over the deck's rail, peering down into the foamy sea. Perhaps her spirit is intact. She breathes deeply and closes her eyes, aware of her galloping pulse, her grumbling stomach, her whirling thoughts. She believes her spirit is of one piece, reasonably whole, quietly yearning, ethereal and unknowable, hanging inside her and flapping against her heart.

They're headed to the Maldives, south of India, to a tiny uninhabited island that apparently can be circled on foot in ten minutes' time. The crew needs to foam-wash the carpets and encourages all passengers to go ashore or assemble in the Diamond Lady Lounge for a day of Bingo. Eve packs a small bag with her bikini bottoms and two condoms. She wears a bikini top and a fluttery wrap that swishes against her ankles and feels silky against her naked ass. It'll be all right. How she wants Adam with his dark, expressive eyes, like a deer trapped in headlights.

The ship's tenders take them to the uninhabited island, which has a public address system and plumbing. They stand in the barbecue line with their respective mothers, listening to "Surfin' U.S.A." over the P.A. "Hey, sexy," Adam whispers into Eve's ear, "I can see your ass through that skirt. Can you ditch your mom?"

Eve nods and grins. "Can you ditch yours?" she whispers back.

"Right after I get my soy dog."

Eve and her mom sway to the music with the other passengers as they munch on hot dogs. Slowly Eve wanders away and pretends to take a stroll. Once she's out of eyesight she hightails it around the tiny island, reaching into her backpack and tearing open the condom wrapper.

She sees Adam hightailing it toward her from the opposite direction. They run and embrace. Eve suddenly feels shy beneath the sunshine. Adam pulls her behind a shrub and yanks off her bikini top.

"Not so fast."

"In about five minutes this place is going to be crawling with senior citizens."

"Tell me something nice," she coos. "Something sexy."

"Do you want to do it or not?" he asks.

"Of course."

They undress and lie on Eve's wrap and have a quickie, a hot, sweaty quickie while Eve squints into the sun. When it's over, they lie for a moment like corpses, tangled together. Then Adam pulls out and rolls off the condom. They kneel naked in the sand, fumbling with their bathing suits.

"That's one way to do it," Eve says with a small smile.

"Sorry," Adam says.

"No, no," Eve says.

"You all right?"

"Uh-huh."

They hear voices and quickly get dressed and fling themselves into the sea. Fellow passengers stream past them. Some wave. Eve is relieved when Adam swims over and takes her wet hand. "Let's go back," he says.

"And here I'm thinking you're swimming over to whisper sweet nothings in my ear."

"Sweet," he whispers into her hair. "Nothings."

Eve changes back into her wrap skirt while Adam pockets the gooey, sandy condom. Slowly, they start to back away from each other in the directions from which they came.

"See ya," Eve says.

"Later," Adam says.

Facing each other, they creep backwards until Eve wonders who will turn away first. It will be her, she's ready to turn. Seconds pass, but she doesn't turn. She becomes very still. If she turns away now she might miss what's supposed to happen next.

It's Adam who turns with a quick wave of his hand. Eve watches him grow smaller as he jogs away.

Adam has beaten her back to the other end of the island. He's brought reading material and lounges under a palm tree. Eve sits with her mom, who's baking under the sun, and they watch Adam slap at the insect circling his head.

"I thought hippies had gone out of vogue," her mother murmurs.

"Hippies are timeless," Eve says and sighs.

"They don't make a lot of money."

"Oh Jesus, Mom."

"I want a grandchild," her mother says. "I just think you're barking up the wrong tree with that one. He probably doesn't have much of a pot to piss in."

"How romantic!"

"*Romance?*" her mother says. "You're almost thirty years old. You need a husband."

"I'm having some *fun* here!" Eve yells.

"You don't look like you're having fun," her mom says.

Adam is still swatting the air. He flutters both hands before spinning away in a tizzy. Eve marches over to him and slaps the torturous mosquito against his forehead, leaving a bloody smudge.

"Fuck!" Adam says.

She realizes then how pissed off she is, not specifically, but generally; she's a very pissed-off person. She flicks the mosquito away.

At dusk the crew builds a bonfire and the passengers form a single-file line and bunny-hop around the flames. The sky is pink and soft, beckoning. Eve gazes into it, transfixed by its perfect beauty and indifference, until she is forced to join the bunny-hopping line, holding onto the fleshy middle of the old man in front of her as they hop across the sand. There they are—fools and bunny-hoppers—hooting and hollering under a glorious sky.

Adam and Eve take the last tender back to the ship. They smile too widely at each other, and for the first time since she's met him, which seems a long time ago, she can't think of anything to say. As they climb onto the floating dock to board the ship, Eve's aware of her naked ass beneath her wrap. Looking back at the tiny island, she realizes she's left her bikini bottom behind.

Later when Adam and Eve meet up in the Water Hole, he is morose and fiddles with the olive in his martini. He hunkers down in his seat and complains about his depreciating Oppenheimer account and one of his exes, who is a ratfink. He gazes too long at the beautiful Asian waitress who brings them fresh drinks. As Eve gets buzzed on fuzzy navels, Adam begins to look strange to her. His head seems perfectly round and he wears the loose-lipped look of a moron. How has she not seen this until now? Adam is a stupid bore. He drones on and on until she screams into his ear, "We're on the Arabian Sea, for Christ's sake. *The Arabian Sea!*"

He looks at her, alarmed. "Chill," he says.

She lets the anger rattle around inside her for a minute, realizing that the air and the sea and the light have seduced them, conspired with them, pushed them toward this moment, toward nothing at all.

What's clear is that Adam is a mostly nice guy who's got some issues and is ultimately not the one; what's also clear is that she's not yet ready to know. So she clings, literally, to his arm, pawing him, while they get sloshed in the Water Hole beneath the stars.

Why has love eluded me? she wonders. Love is such a natural thing, after all. Is she too ridiculous, too cranky, too old, too set in her ways, too lusty, small-minded, immature? Other ridiculous people have found love, like her co-worker Lucy with the sleepy mascara-crusted eyes, who's addicted to "Drama in Real Life!" stories in *Reader's Digest*. Slurping her drink, Eve gazes up at the night sky—so high above her head—and thinks, *when will it be my turn? Mine.*

They dock in India, in the port of Goa, and Eve ditches everybody. She ditches her mom, who's visiting Portuguese cathedrals, and Adam, who's visiting

Hindu temples, and Adam's mom, who's going shopping in Panjim. Instead, Eve hires a taxi and goes to the beach, where cows lie on the red sand looking soulfully at the waves.

Eve hasn't lost anything. It's not her own spirit that concerns her, it's Adam's which has attached itself to hers. His ghostly residue is as useless and cumbersome as an extra foot. He's living inside her, infecting her dreams, her thoughts, her every second. That's the way it is with Eve. It's an ancient story. How she wishes she could knock him out with the heel of her hand, like water from her ear.

So she does what she can. She spends the day swimming in the Arabian Sea, bobbing in the waves. She walks along the shoreline and catches glimpses of shells as the tide rolls out. Digging, she discovers finger-long snail shells—purple and gold—slender tornadoes. Some are broken, most are perfect. Such treasures. As the light begins to change, she lies on the sand near the cows while her taxi driver sits on the hood of the car, reading the newspaper.

Later she asks him to drive, to just drive. They ride through twisty tree-lined lanes. She stares out at houses the colors of Easter eggs, where chickens, dogs and cows wander through yards. Sparkly clothes hang on clotheslines and catch the last of the light. The taxi zooms with the windows wide open,

and the flotsam of Adam embedded in her crocodile
brain begins to shed itself like dandelion fluff until
she imagines she might be free and clear.

STEW

MRS. ALLARD CALLED J.D.'S MOTHER EARLIER IN THE
day and asked if he could babysit since their regular
girl had the flu. His mom said, of course.

"Ah, Ma," he groaned, when he came through
the back door and she told him the news.

"Have a heart, J.D. honey. They're stuck, and
they're going to some kind of dinner party," his mom
said, looking delighted, the way she often looked,
even now as she rooted through the refrigerator,
opening lids and sniffing brown saucy things.

J.D. wasn't sure he ever looked delighted. In
recent Christmas photos he noticed he looked glazed,
not with boredom exactly, but with something dull
and gloomy, and he wondered about his mother, radi-
ating goodness and luck. He stuffed a Twinkie in his

mouth and thought about objecting to the babysitting, but he liked the idea of getting out of the house.

"It's money in your pocket," his mom said.

"I'll be loaded," he said with his mouth full. "All right. I'll do it," he added, as if he had the final say.

J.D. had occasionally babysat the girls, Annabel and Sophia, when the Allards lived next door. But last year they had left their three-bedroom ranch and moved across town to—according to nosy neighbors—a tiny two-bedroom on a lumpy piece of property, and J.D. hadn't seen one of the downwardly mobile Allards since. J.D. was now a high school freshman with bad skin and a meager social life and no real Friday evening options; sometimes he'd go to one of his friends' houses and they'd listen to music and toss a tennis ball against the wall, passing the time. Soccer was his thing, but it was January and the streets and tree branches glinted with ice.

J.D. plopped in front of the TV and stared at an old black-and-white movie. The remote didn't work and since he was too lazy to get up and change the channel, he watched a young woman with a hairdo in the shape of an ocean wave embrace a young man under a street lamp. "I would do anything for it not to be true," the man said, pulling away from her and holding his hat over his heart. "But what we had here is over, dollface. We're through." J.D. watched their eyes glisten, he saw their sadness. He had his own little storage bin of strange, sad feelings he tried to keep under lock and key. He felt something like heartache when he thought about the mysterious girls, walking the hallways of his school. There were so many new faces since the graduated eighth graders from both the town's junior highs and at least half of the Catholic school spilled together to make up the freshman class. His drama class was filled with many of these exotic girls. There was Susan Steen with her magical hair. He had watched her pull on one of her tight curls, pulling it past her shoulder to almost her elbow and when she let it go it sprung back up to half its length. There was Katie Taylor, who he heard danced ballet. Her spine was straight and her neck long, and even though she was a little chubby, when she walked nothing jiggled. There was Luann Morley, who still had a child's body and a loud, high laugh. She could do a cartwheel on the balance beam. One day after school he walked by the gym and saw her strong arms stretched taut on the beam as her little legs parted in the air, and then as if her legs had eyes they landed to safety, one chalky foot after the other. She wobbled only the tiniest bit. He wondered about all these girls and what they were like to talk to. What did they think about? Would he ever know? Thinking like this was sometimes delicious, sometimes terrible.

He hadn't wanted drama class; he wanted shop,

where they made tool racks and bar stools, but fresh-
men got leftovers and he was rerouted to the arts. "A
thespian," the old guidance counselor shouted in
J.D.'s ear, handing him his schedule. It would have
been intolerable if it weren't for these girls who filled
the seats in front of him. From his seat in the back of
the room, he could stare, unseen, at the back of their
fine heads and wonder about them.

Two weeks ago, the drama teacher had asked the
class to form groups, choose a play from the shelves,
and present a scene. J.D. sat quietly, waiting for one
of these girls to turn to him, which they were bound
to do considering he was one of only three boys in the
class; there were boy parts, he knew. But this didn't
seem to matter. He watched as desks were turned and
groups sprung up. He watched and waited and found
himself alone.

Then Dawn Martinelli poked him in the arm. "I
guess you're stuck with me," she said.

"I am?" Dawn Martinelli was a big, beefy girl
with bad skin, like his, although her pimples were red
and mean and gathered in small clusters, while he
had a couple of large, sluggish bumps. He knew
Dawn Martinelli's type, from her chicken soup smell
to her huffy attitude. He had her pegged.

"You'll be Vladimir and I'll be this Estragon,"
she said, thrusting a copy of *Waiting for Godot* at
him. "We'll do this scene where they call each other

names. 'You abortion! You sewer rat!'"

"You lobotomy," he whispered.

"You butthole," she said. He inched his chair away from hers, looking at the gray sky. January was one of those months that went on forever.

"We'll be bums. It'll be wicked. You'll see," she said.

J.D.'s mom dropped him off at the Allards' at seven o'clock. The house was small and bright with a yellow living room, a little yellow kitchen and a short yellow hallway, sprouting two bedrooms and a bathroom, which were probably yellow as well, J.D. thought. "John Dewey, how are you?" Mrs. Allard smiled. She was cheerful and dumpy, wearing pink lipstick.

The kitchen table had been moved into the living room and a rickety card table was pushed up next to it. Both tables were covered with a paper tablecloth. Six assorted chairs were gathered around the tables, and each place was set with a bowl, a spoon, and a napkin. Mr. Allard in his coat and boots carefully placed a dish of melting butter to the right of the bread basket, then the left. "Where do you think, Johnny?" Mr. Allard asked, when he saw J.D. watching him. J.D. shrugged.

"Girls, girls, John Dewey is here," Mrs. Allard called.

Shy at first, Annabel and Sophia clung together and whispered into each other's hair. They wore flannel nightgowns and plaid slippers. Annabel was eight and could be a chatterbox. J.D. remembered her once standing on his shoes and holding his hands, discussing nimbostratus clouds; she and J.D. had dazzled each other with the weather report. Sophia was younger and quieter and had dark, dark eyes. Both girls had chin-length hair and mild cases of static electricity. A couple strands rose, almost elegantly, toward the ceiling.

"We're having a progressive dinner, J.D. We'll come back here for stew." The Allards grabbed their coats, kissed the girls and left. For the first half-hour, the girls colored quietly on the floor, looking up at him shyly, then looking away. "It's been a long time since we saw you, John Dewey," Annabel said after a while.

"J.D.," he said.

"Oh."

"Do you want a snack?" he asked.

"We had our snack," Annabel said.

J.D. settled on the couch, opened *Waiting for Godot* and studied his lines. He'd finally agreed to it because he wanted the class to notice him, notice that he was breathing the same air as they were in the same overheated classroom; he hoped the scene would be funny, and he found he liked yelling insults at Dawn Martinelli. Earlier in the week, though,

when they were supposed to be rehearsing their
scene, Dawn Martinelli had stared out the window
and wouldn't cooperate.

"What's the matter with you?" he asked.

"I decided to stop talking so much. I'm trying to
cultivate a sense of mystery."

"Well, you'll still be weird and boring."

"I'm not boring," she said mildly.

"No," he agreed. Boring wasn't one of her flaws.
"But this is required talking."

Dawn pointed to one of the groups. "They're
doing *The Effects of Gamma Rays on Man-in-the-
Moon Marigolds.*"

"Who?"

"You don't know a thing about art, do you?" she
said, leaning her fat head close to him and scowling.

"Get out of my face," he said, inching his desk
away.

"You are so blah," she said, lightly, almost musi-
cally. "There's not one thing about you that's memo-
rable. You could disintegrate right now and not one
person in this room would notice."

He felt himself get warm, could feel his face red-
dening. They seemed to instinctively know things
about each other that he wished they didn't know. "I
take it back," he said, as easily as he could. "You *are*
boring." But he could see they'd both gotten under
one another's skin, and for the rest of the week they

spent third period drama class alternately rehearsing their lines and saying terrible things to each other.

Now just looking at the lines made his heart sink. He didn't know what to make of high school, where he walked the halls like a phantom. He closed his eyes for a moment and then looked over at the Allard girls, who were watching him expectantly. They smiled, looked down into their coloring books, and then looked up again.

"Annie Fofannie, Sophster," he said, suddenly, tossing aside the book. "Let's have some fun."

The girls jumped to their feet. First they played Evil Baby Snatcher—an escaped jailbird who was as slippery as smoke, passing under doors and through cracks, tried to enter the Allard home and seize the girls. The girls had to spot Evil Baby Snatcher before it got a stranglehold on one of their little necks. Sophia would point to the shadowy, lurking snatcher while Annabel bugged out her eyes and let herself come close to death by asphyxiation. J.D.'s job was to wind up his pitching arm and send Evil Baby Snatcher sailing through the window and out onto the telephone pole, where they would listen closely and try to decipher its evil words and prepare themselves for the next attack. Next, they played Smokers, a game where they sucked on pretend cigarettes and hacked their brains out and talked in raspy voices.

Then the girls dragged two boxes that were each

marked $1 into the living room. "We got this junk at a rummage sale," Annabel said. Inside one box were many pairs of dress shoes, now old and crunched and dusty. The other box held hats and purses and accessories. All of it smelled liked someone's basement.

Annabel flipped through the stuff and draped herself in a fox wrap—the old, sad, toothed head sat on one shoulder and its ratty tail hung off the other. She wore a beaded beret and pointy-toed satin slippers. J.D. found a beat-up motorbike helmet and goggles.

"Miss Vanilla Bean," he said, getting down on one knee. "I would do anything for it not to be true, but what we had here is over."

"Noooooooo," Annabel said, throwing herself onto the recliner, writhing and moaning, her nightgown twisting around her pale legs. "You have to staaaaay…"

"I'm sorry," J.D. said. "We're kaput."

She threw herself at J.D.'s feet, her mouth opening and searching for words. "But tomorrow it will be sunny, a warm front is moving in and we might make it to the low fifties." He shook his head sorrowfully.

In the meantime, Sophia had slipped a dirty pink boa around her neck. She wore a Peter Pan cap with a feather shooting off to the side and glittery pumps. In her hands she held an alligator purse.

"Miss Horseradish, I wish it weren't true," J.D.

said, holding the helmet over his heart. "But what we had here is over."

Sophia looked shy, standing on the carpet in her getup.

"We're all washed up," J.D. urged.

"Act!" Annabel yelled.

Sophia looked stricken, and she just stood there clutching the alligator purse. They waited, and finally Sophia gave a dramatic turn of her head and teetered in her high heels over to the closet, opened the door, stepped inside among the fishing poles and overcoats and slammed herself in.

"Well," Annabel said. "That's not really acting."

"It was pretty darn good."

"*Really?*" Annabel shouted.

"Really," J.D. said.

They stared at the closet door, waiting for Sophia to reappear. Slowly, the door opened and Sophia, red as a beet, came stumbling out. J.D. applauded, and she smiled hugely, pulling on her Peter Pan cap and making the jaunty feather point skyward.

Then the girls changed into new getups and paraded around the living room, walking the runway. "Work it, girls," he said.

At 8:30 when it was their bedtime, J.D. sent the girls to the bathroom to brush their teeth. He looked in their little bedroom, stuffed with dolls, board games and miniature kitchen appliances. They had bunk beds covered with brightly flowered blankets.

"Let us stay up late. Come on, John Dewey," Annabel said.

"No, no." He leaned in the bathroom doorway as the girls took turns spitting into the sink. "Goodnight, little ones, goodnight. Tonight the moon shines high and the lamp light glows, goodnight little ones, goodnight," he said. This was something his grandmother had said to him when he was small. He could still imagine the watery potato smell of her kitchen, and for a second he was overcome with great love for her; she'd been gone for a long time. He backed into the hall, missing his grandmother and her house built on stilts with its ramps and staircases and the view of the sea. He swallowed hard. "Vamoose," he said, pointing to their bedroom. "Kapeesh?"

The girls climbed into their beds and pulled the covers up, looking at him standing in the doorway. "We had fun, didn't we?" Annabel said.

He nodded, then felt stupid and weird. He closed their door and returned to the couch, wondering if he was still that same boy who had run up the ramps and staircases of his grandmother's house on stilts, or whether he had grown up. After he and Dawn Martinelli had insulted each other one day this week, he'd taken a hall pass and went to the bathroom, where he examined his face. He squeezed a pimple, making the skin raw. He ran his fingers under the cold water and thought about peeing, but he didn't really have to. When he returned to class the room buzzed with unfamiliar voices. He heard Katie Taylor croon, "I've had many gentlemen callers." Lynn Cooper whispered, "Oh Brick, sometimes I feel like a cat on a hot tin roof," and Susan Steen yelled in a trembly voice, "STELLA...STELLA!" In the short time he'd been gone, everyone in the room had become someone else.

J.D. heard a car crunch over the ice, and the headlights filled the living room for a second. Nine o'clock, he saw on the wall clock. Two hours, six bucks. He reached for his jacket, working his long arms into the sleeves.

Mr. and Mrs. Allard dashed in with their coats flying open and waved at him before disappearing into the kitchen. Next, a large woman heaved herself through the door and headed for the card table, where she sat down and buttered herself a piece of bread, still wearing her coat. A man in a furry hat with earflaps and big glasses walked in soon after and asked J.D. directions to the bathroom, and he was followed by an elderly couple—the old man, tall and stooped, moved slowly into the room and folded his coat across the back of the couch while his birdlike wife stood on the welcome mat. "Let me help you with your galoshes, dear," he said to her.

"Why?" she asked. "I'm just going to have to put them back on."

J.D. stood in the middle of the room, waiting for one of the swift-moving Allards to pay him and drive him home. It smelled good in the kitchen, and he felt his stomach growl. The large, bread-eating woman patted crumbs from her lips with a napkin and wandered into the kitchen.

"What are we eating?" Birdy asked, still standing on the welcome mat.

"Stew, I believe," the old man said, lowering himself into a folding chair.

"We had soup at that Phipps fellow's," she said, gesturing toward the bathroom.

"What can I say?" the old man said quietly.

"How many bowls of soup do they think I can eat?"

"Shush, dear."

Mrs. Allard entered the living room with a bottle of red wine and stopped short, seeing J.D. in his jacket. "Oh, J.D., we're not taking you home yet. Didn't we tell you? This is a progressive dinner. You see, we had coconut soup at Mr. Phipps's," she said, referring to the bathroom man who had just returned to the living room. "And cheese puffs and pigs-in-a-blanket at Mrs. Martinelli's. We'll have beef stew here and then we're off to the Waverlys' for cheesecake and a lemon-lime sherbet roll." Mrs. Waverly, the birdlike woman, offered half a smile and held up her wineglass for Mrs. Allard to fill. "Everyone, this is J.D., the babysitter," Mrs. Allard said, and the room turned to him.

J.D. lifted his hand stiffly in more of a stop signal than a greeting. *Mrs. Martinelli*, he thought queasily. He searched her face for hints of Dawn and sure enough he found them in her high, flat forehead, her large frame, the way she moved her mouth. J.D. backed up a few paces, still standing in his jacket while the dinner guests moved around him. They expected him to sit on the couch while they ate their beef stew. What did they think he should do with himself while they ate their beef stew? And what if it somehow got back to Dawn that he was a babysitter, a Friday night babysitter? He grew warm and anxious, standing on the yellow carpeting. There wasn't anywhere for him to sit other than the couch, so he sat on the farthest end and unzipped his jacket. He took his book out of his pocket and nervously turned the pages.

"Hey, Johnny boy, do you mind if I flip the light for some atmosphere?" Mr. Allard asked, though he didn't wait for a response. Mr. Allard was red-faced and chatty from the wine. He turned off the lamp, and the little room was filled with soft candlelight.

Mr. and Mrs. Allard scooped stew into bowls and poured more wine, after which the bathroom man

said a short prayer. J.D. sat in the dimness, pretending to read. A progressive dinner party was one of the
dumbest ideas he'd ever heard. Coconut soup over
here and cheese puffs over there while babysitters
were made to sit on the couch, eavesdropping. And
just how was the dinner "progressive," just what was
the point? Where did they think they would arrive?
A lemon-lime sherbet log was hardly a prize, hardly
something to work up to.

J.D. half-listened as the dinner guests discussed a
sermon from the previous Sunday, Saturday morning
traffic jams on Main Street, and each of their paper-
boys, who were of the same ilk, haphazardly tossing
the day's news into the snow. J.D. stifled a yawn and
listened to his stomach grumble. He almost wished
he'd been offered a bowl of stew. He stole glances at
the guests, then looked away. He slid out of his jacket and shifted uncomfortably.

"My Dawn has her first boyfriend," Mrs.
Martinelli said. "Vladimir."

"A Russian?" the old man asked.

"Possibly."

J.D. sat up as if plugged in. His entire head
warmed. He glanced at the dinner guests until he
realized no one was paying attention to him, and then
he closed his book and stared.

"She talks about him constantly. She says he's
nuts about her."

"Oh, to be a teenager again!" Mrs. Allard said.

"Teenagers can be a pain in the ass though," Birdy said. The room quieted except for the sound of spoons clinking against bowls.

"Everyone's a pain in the ass on occasion," the old man said.

There were murmurs of agreement.

"I'm glad about this Vladimir," Mrs. Martinelli said. "Dawn just started high school and I worry about her. She's never had many friends and she's moody and she's getting fat, like I should talk." She eyed the potato on her spoon. "You know how those years can be. It can feel like being on the outside looking in, waiting for something to happen." She slid the potato into her mouth and held it there.

"It can feel like you're always waiting for something," Mr. Allard said.

Mrs. Allard looked at her husband for a quick second and attempted a laugh. J.D. studied the dinner guests so closely he might have been watching a movie. He watched the way the old man nodded his saggy-cheeked head in agreement, the way the bathroom man gazed from one person's face to the next with his magnified eyes, the way Birdy nibbled on her bread, thinking. They were polite in the way strangers were, yet they seemed to understand each other, too. J.D. felt exhilarated, thinking that Dawn Martinelli had made a boyfriend out of Vladimir, a fiery character from a play on the dusty shelves in their classroom. She told her mother about this pretend boyfriend. She invented stories. He could see there were things Dawn wanted, too—things she didn't yet have. It was also possible that she liked J.D. He let these thoughts, which weren't unpleasant but strange and mysterious, scramble around inside his head. Slowly, he began to feel a friendly pity for Dawn Martinelli and the Allards, too, and as he sat there he began to feel a friendly pity for himself.

"Luckily," Mrs. Allard said, brightly, "we have some time before Annabel and Sophia are ready for boyfriends."

"*Annabel* and *Sophia*," Birdy said. "How grand! Maybe they're destined for great things."

Mr. and Mrs. Allard smiled uneasily, and J.D. could tell that they thought Birdy might be making fun of them. He saw it in their eyes. He didn't know how he knew, but he knew the Allards had great hopes for their girls. J.D. also knew Birdy wasn't making fun of anyone, and he had an urge, like an itch, to straighten it out. He searched the Allards' faces to see if he'd misread them, but they sat stiffly on their folding chairs, spooning beef stew up to their mouths. The Allards were grown people with sleeping children down the hall. It was disturbing to think he understood something they didn't.

Then Annabel poked her head into the living

room, with her finger to her lips. She gestured for
J.D. to come to her. He slipped off the couch and
rounded the table of dinner guests, who ignored him,
and made his way down the hall to the bathroom,
where Annabel sat glumly on the rim of the tub. She
had a crust of sleep in her eye.

"I was thinking," she said. "Maybe next time I
could pop out of the closet. I could say 'I have traveled so far!' I could wear the goggles and helmet.
Wouldn't that be good?"

J.D. smiled at her. "You could say, 'Let me tell
you about the places I've been and the things I've
seen.'"

"Oh!" she said, thinking of possibilities.

It was clear there was nothing Annabel needed.
She just wanted to talk with someone and be up past
her bedtime, this little girl in her flannel nightgown.

"Why aren't you sitting at the table with them?"
she asked.

"I'm the babysitter."

"So you just sit on the couch?"

"Yup."

She stood on the rim of the tub and raised the
window. Cold air blew in. It had started to snow, and
the wind swirled the flakes against the darkness.
"Tomorrow a cold pocket of air is coming down from
Canada and we could get..." She shrugged. "Four
feet of snow!"

He stood next to her and looked out the window. She was fibbing. Tomorrow a warm front would move into the area, and it was expected that the temperature would rise for the next few days at least.

TRUE

IT WAS HARD HAVING A LOUSY PERSONALITY. Robin would rather have been cursed with a weight problem or a bald spot or thick glasses, or better yet a missing finger. Instead she was stuck with her personality, which was a non-personality, a blank sheet of paper she kept trying to write on. Case in point: here it was Friday night, and she was hiding out in some little kid's bedroom pretending to care for Lila, who was a slut and was passed out on the gingham bedspread with chunks of puke dotted down the front of her shirt, while downstairs a party went on without them.

It was becoming boring, sitting on the bed and staring at Lila, who breathed rhythmically through her slack mouth, putting Robin into a stupor. Robin

moved to the corner of the bedroom, where a naked
Barbie doll was spread-eagled over the breakfast
nook of the beach bungalow. Robin dressed the doll
in a fringy cowgirl outfit and was deciding between
boots or Jesus sandals when her friend Janet popped
into the room, guzzling from a bottle of wine.

"What are you *doing*?" Janet said.

"Lila's sick here."

"Lila's a slut," Janet said. "Why are you hiding?
Have *you* talked to three new people?"

Robin set the Barbie doll on the roof of the beach
house, placing the sleek, smiling head up against the
Barbie telescope, which was aimed at the lavender
wallpaper beyond which were the hedges where
Robin had parked her bike an hour earlier. In her
mind's eye, she could see the bike there, awaiting her.

"The thing is—" Robin said.

"What? Speak up!"

"It's just that parties—"

"Oh, I know what you're going to say: 'I don't
like parties.' But if you don't like parties then you
can't really like people and if you don't like people
then you're an antisocial."

"I like people."

Janet sighed. She was a junior and a year older
than Robin. She had an underbite and would have
her jaw broken, realigned, and wired shut one day in
the distant future. She was the first and only friend

Robin had made when Robin's family moved here last year. Janet, who worked on the yearbook and school spirit committees, had knocked on her door last summer just days after Robin's family had moved in and had taken Robin on a walking tour of downtown. "Here's Friendly's, where you can get a chocolate Fribble," she'd said. "Lots of kids hang out here. I mean it's fine when you're in eighth grade but when you're our age it just sucks, bites, and blows. Here's the movie theater where the floor's as flat as a pancake. They've been showing a lot of love stories, which are my favorites, but if you get a large head in front of you it just sucks, bites, and blows. Here's Trimmings Salon where, trust me, all you'll want to do is get a trim. If you're looking for a new hairdo you'll have to get your butt on New Jersey Transit and head into the city. God, you have gorgeous hair," she said, grabbing a handful of Robin's long, dark hair and holding it up to her own head. "My hair's decent but some days..." She rolled her eyes up to the True Value Hardware sign, which glared green above them. "Isn't this place the worst?"

Janet now plunked down on the bed next to Lila and stared hard at Robin for several seconds. "It makes me so unhappy, Robin, that you won't try to be a more popular person."

Robin reached for Janet's bottle and sipped long and hard. The wine tasted like rotten fruit—overly

sweet and funky—and thinking this made her start to
gag and she handed back the bottle.

"Listen, I hate to be boring," Janet said in a low
voice, "but there are some things you obviously don't
know." She looked up to the ceiling, as if thinking,
and from where Robin was sitting on the floor Janet's
underbite looked really, really bad. "We live in a
highly structurized society," Janet began. "Friends
don't grow on trees. You can't go *pluck* one. You
have to make friends. If you just set a little goal to talk
to three new people tonight that could be three more
friends for you. Don't you see? It's not enough to be
pretty and just stare into space. You have to act the
right way. I've had to work at developing my excellent personality." Janet slid onto the floor next to
Robin, her boobs jiggling into place. "Take Lila
here," she whispered, pointing up to the bed. "If she
fooled around like a normal person she'd be fine. But
no, she's so obvious that everyone knows her business and so she's just a slut. *Bor*-ing. I mean, who
wants to be her friend? Well, I'm her friend, but you
know what I mean. I'm going to be honest because I
care about you, Robin; the thing is that sometimes
you can be embarrassing...I haven't hurt your feelings, have I?" She looked at Robin deeply. Janet had
enormous eyes fringed with sparse, stubby lashes;
they were the eyes of a strange, graceful sea creature
gliding peaceably over coral reefs.

Robin quickly shook her head. In Janet's presence, she often felt slow and clumsy as the sparky shower of Janet's words rained down on her. Now she found herself jittery with gratitude and rage. "I can talk to three people."

"See," Janet said. "Really, I'm just trying to help."

"Thank you, Janet."

Janet nodded. Then she stood and frowned at Lila and wandered toward the door. "Coming?" she asked.

"Yep," Robin said, unable to move.

"Good," Janet said, disappearing into the hallway.

Go, Robin told herself. *Go now*, she commanded, otherwise she might be afflicted with her lousy personality for the rest of her life. She stared at Lila, who was snoring into the kid's pillow. Yes, Lila was a little sloppy and slutty but she also had a zesty life. *Be a normal girl*, she commanded herself. Growing angrier, she loped down the hall and down the stairs until she found herself in the middle of the party surrounded by a roomful of lively kids, holding beer cans and waving cigarettes and talking, talking, talking. Robin's anger instantly fled her body, and she felt deserted, standing there with a dried-out mouth and a twitchy eye. Directly in front of her was a loveseat. She made a beeline for it but two senior girls beat her to it, and she teetered for a second. A wall, a wall; she needed a wall. She quickly moved to the corner of the room, where she sat on the arm of a couch and let her hair fall over her face like a dark curtain. Then she waited for what might happen.

"Are you sleeping?" a guy sitting on the couch asked, giving her a poke.

"Nope," Robin said, opening her eyes.

"Just checking."

Robin smiled, feeling herself blush and grow warm. The guy turned back to the girl beside him, cocking his head and grinning as she twirled a strand of hair around her finger. They were having a conversation in which they said things like, "I did not," "Yes, you did," "When?" "Come on, you know." They kept at it for the longest time and Robin wondered how these bits of nothing, like dust, kept the two of them tied up with each other for so long. Soon they wandered away, and Robin realized that if she just sat here, in the corner, on the arm of the couch, she'd be all right.

A girl across the room who had been furiously whispering with two other girls veered toward Robin's couch and plunked down. She looked like a fly. She had short black hair that hugged her head like a helmet and heavy eyelids, and Robin had often seen her zipping down the halls at school. She now turned to Robin and said in a low voice, "Would you be friends with someone who called you an asshole for no reason?"

"I definitely wouldn't," Robin said, elated. She

slid off the arm of the couch to sit beside the girl.

"Well, I wouldn't either...but I don't want to talk about it."

"Who called you an asshole for no reason?" Robin whispered into the girl's ear, which wasn't very clean.

"It's very discouraging," the fly went on, "when you're the type of person who goes out of your way to do nice things for your friends and you learn that one of them doesn't even give two little shits about your feelings. I call that very discouraging."

It sounded very discouraging. Maybe she and this fly could be friends, Robin thought. "I bet it was the redhead," Robin whispered. "She looks like a creep."

The fly turned to her head-on. "Not *her*. The *other* one."

"Oh," Robin said.

"It's very discouraging to hear you call my very best friend creepy." The girl gave her a fishy look, popped off the couch and returned to her little circle.

Robin sat there, trying not to stare at anyone and hoping no one was staring at her. Then George from her geometry class joined her on the couch, tapping his foot to Nirvana. He had the bluest eyes, so blue you couldn't help but think he was a nice person, even if he was stoned most of the time. "Robin!" he said and smiled. She smiled back. He held out his hand, fingers splayed, and for a panicky second she didn't know what he wanted her to do. He didn't seem to be looking for a high five. Did he want to shake, or what? He was stoned, she could see that. He had a rubber band around his wrist. She had the urge to flick it. A little flick. She would've liked to do that, but somehow couldn't. He took back his hand and looked at her funny, and then he was tapping his foot again, and the moment was gone. George bounded off the couch and disappeared into the room.

Well, Robin thought, that was three, sort of: the guy who asked her if she was sleeping, the fly, and George from geometry. She headed downstairs where it was darker, louder, and more crowded and stood next to Janet, who was talking to Nolan Fry. Nolan Fry was the prettiest person in the entire school. He had smooth pink skin, a flop of dirty blond hair hanging over his forehead, and he was very tall. Every feature—his thin nose, full lips, heavy eyelashes—was perfect in and of itself, but, as Janet had often said, all together on the same face was almost a crime. It was hard, Robin decided, to look at him head on. Worse yet, he knew *how* to be pretty. He wore his prettiness like a smart jacket. Janet was staring up at him as if in a trance; her eyes had gone soft and she wore the faintest smile while Nolan talked to the air above her head. Neither one of them looked at Robin, but when she reached for the wine bottle Janet released her grip. Robin gulped and when she handed it back, Janet's fingers expertly closed around the bottle. Robin wished she knew how to be pretty the way Nolan did. She'd only recently become pretty and often needed to look in the bathroom mirror to be reminded. She slipped through the sliding doors into the cold air, where she got on her bike and raced home.

They had a drug problem at school. Lots of kids smoked pot, but it seemed they also had some sniffers who inhaled stuff like Drano and paint thinner. The school now held weekly seminars in the auditorium ever since one jerky sophomore had suffered some brain damage. Everyone plodded into the auditorium, weary and dead-eyed. Janet waved to Robin and pointed to the seat she'd saved her.

This week's seminar featured a dramatization of several kids gathered in a bathroom while Britney Spears' "Oops!…I Did It Again" played in the background. One of the actors played a reluctant kid, who sat on the lid of the toilet bowl while several other actors tried to pressure him into putting a plastic bag over his head and sniffing some Aquanet hairspray.

Janet scribbled on a piece of notebook paper and handed it to Robin. "I think U R too dependent on me," it read.

The lights dimmed, the actors froze and a voice from outer space said, "Rule number one: Think of your future. Remember your hopes and dreams.

Brain damage is not cool!"

"Exasperating!" Janet whispered. "If you're a big enough moron to sniff hairspray, then you should get brain damage."

The actors unfroze and the reluctant one said, "Hey, listen, sniffing household substances isn't cool. They can mess up your head. I have algebra homework, and in a couple of years I'm going to college."

Robin underlined the words "too dependent" and scribbled, "How?" She stared at Janet's profile, waiting.

"Not any 1 thing," Janet wrote. "HOW can a ♀ go thru h.s. w/ only 1 friend?"

The actor who wouldn't sniff the Aquanet leapt off the toilet seat lid, and a spotlight zeroed in on him. The outer space voice said, "Cool Kid." Cool Kid smiled broadly and donned a graduation cap and then galloped offstage. The outer space voice then said, "Jackasses." The spotlight zoomed in on the hairspray sniffers, who were wearing donkey ears and braying as they wielded the Aquanet and pulled plastic bags over their heads and banged into the toilet and the tub. There were snickers and yawns. *Lame,* a boy behind them called out.

"What do I do?" Robin wrote, feeling herself go clammy.

"I don't have all the answers," Janet whispered. "I definitely don't." She gave Robin a small, weary smile, revealing her bottom row of even white teeth.

Every week during the seminars they got a new pamphlet and this week's said, "Everybody Wants to Be Cool and That's Okay." Robin read a list of ways to be cool. Help a disadvantaged child; be a good neighbor. Doing something for a kid or neighbor was certainly nice but it wasn't cool, she thought. Who were these people to talk about cool when they didn't know what it was either? The room was filled with the whish of pamphlets hitting the auditorium floor. Janet flicked hers, and it ricocheted off the seat in front of her before landing next to their feet.

Robin was saving the pamphlets. They were a mystery, not really helpful but occasionally very interesting. Last week's—"Reach Out for Friends Not Drugs"—said only a small percentage of the people you meet will actually become friends and that it's important to have realistic expectations. This was a revelation. There were hundreds of kids in the auditorium; there were so many bodies and voices, so similar to each other in their boredom—each of them wiggly and uncomfortable in the stiff seats. Most of us will never really know each other, Robin thought as she looked at the rows and rows of heads in front of her. When Janet wasn't looking Robin slid the pamphlet into her notebook.

Robin sat in the library after school, trying to do geometry homework. She sometimes imagined herself marching over to Janet's house and ending their friendship. She knew Janet would stare deeply into her eyes. Janet would say insulting things—or worse, she might say nothing at all. She might just say "okay" and go back to her little turquoise room at the top of the stairs and apply another coat of Intrigue #39 to her fingernails. It was possible.

Robin soon gave up on the idea and went online to a site she had heard some girls talking about called prettygirl.com. On a message board called "Being Pretty Is Enough," she read:

"I'm kind of a snotty bitch. I like to diddle my boyfriend around and because I'm pretty I CAN. Ha!"

"Don't get me wrong I love being pretty. In fact I'm super pretty but if I had been a little less pretty I might have developed more of a wit. I'm not good at one-liners like my mediocre-looking roommates and sometimes I get jealous, like yesterday when one of them came in with a little flower from the lawn and stuck it in a jelly jar and placed it on the table and said 'weed du jour.' I wish I could come up with stuff like that. I'm twenty so I'm probably older and wiser than most of you. All I'm saying is maybe I should have felt the need to be clever."

And the responses: "I bet she isn't really pretty." "You are so right. I know an ugly girl who reads this website."

Robin thought of the last party and all of the

other terrifying parties Janet had dragged her to. She wrote: "I love that being pretty means I don't have to do anything. People seem to like me just because I'm pretty to look at. Doors open for me wherever I go."

As Robin left the library she saw Nolan Fry, gazing into his locker as if it were a refrigerator. Surprisingly, he was the only one in the hall.

Robin walked toward him. *Doors open for me wherever I go.* "Hi Nolan," she found herself saying.

"Hey," he said, turning his cool eyes on her.

"I thought I'd say 'hi,'" she blurted.

"You're Cheryl."

"Robin."

"Robin," he said, brushing a finger over his lips.

"I'm a sophomore."

He laughed.

"I mean you probably don't know many sophomores, is all."

"Have you read this *Bartleby the Scrivener*?" he asked, pulling it from his locker.

Robin shook her head.

"Bartleby. I like that name," he said, tossing the book into his backpack. He slammed shut his locker. "See ya."

"Bye." He walked the short distance to the side exit. *Doors open for me wherever I go.* Robin stared after him as he left the building. Being pretty hadn't done a damn thing for her. It was almost nothing,

really. She had the urge to check her face in the bathroom mirror.

But Nolan was opening up the door. "Want a
ride?" he called.

She rode in the front seat of Nolan Fry's pickup
truck, which was blue with a slightly crunched passenger door. She was wondering if she should tell him
where she lived or if she should wait for him to ask.
It was easier to look at Nolan's profile than to look at
his dreamy, beautiful face. Nolan apparently didn't
feel the need for chit-chat, and they rode quietly listening to the radio. Every now and then he coughed
and gave his chest a small pound with a fist.

"You're Janet's friend," he said, after a time.

"She's not really my friend," Robin said.

Nolan pulled into the lot at the park and found a
spot under some leafy trees. The sky was growing
dark, and the air had became cool. He took a swig of
the purple cough syrup that lay on the dashboard.
"Want some?" he said.

"Okay," she said. Her mouth had gone dry, and
she took a sip. He laughed and took a joint from his
pocket and rolled it between his fingers. "You
smoke?" he asked.

"Won't that make you cough more?"

"Probably. I'm an idiot sometimes." He took a hit
and handed the joint to her. Robin didn't especially

like getting high, because most times nothing much happened, though once she had the repeated sensation of falling off a curb.

They passed it back and forth until she got a chill and the top of Robin's head went momentarily frosty. Nolan took another swig of cough syrup and slunk down into his seat. Robin felt smooth and polished as a stone and slunk down next to him, and they stared into the park. After a while Nolan said, "Come."

They crawled into the cab of the truck where it smelled like breath and sleep; he lay down on a pile of clothes and she lay next to him. He picked up a chunk of her hair and ran his fingers through it until she tingled all over. He held the strands to his nose. She was aware of how shiny and thick her hair must seem between Nolan's fingers and how lovely she must look. She felt as though she were being revealed to herself for the first time, and she saw a flicker of the alluring girl she could become. Nolan scooted closer and scooped up more of her hair and let it fall over his face. They were like this for a while.

"Janet, man," Nolan said in a sleepy, slow voice. "Do you know she invited me over for lunch last winter?"

"No," Robin barely said.

"This is bizarre..." he whispered, lifting her hair from his face.

"Tell me."

Nolan sat up on his elbows and shook his head as if to clear it. "I'm in the bakery one morning. Janet comes in for a sticky bun and asks me to stop by for lunch. So, I'm like, I guess. I go there expecting grilled cheese...

"When I get there she's the only one home," he said. "She's got the table set in the dining room and she's serving roast tenderloin and mashed potatoes and string beans with almonds. She's got gravy in a gravy boat!

"She's got on tight jeans and all this perfume and high heels. I'm sitting in her freaking dining room with a real napkin, and I'm sweaty and covered in flour. She's running back and forth from the dining room into the kitchen, and her high heels are going click, click, click on the linoleum. The whole time she's smiling like a goon. Man..."

A gravy boat! Robin thought. *High heels!*

"She was seriously hitting on me, man...I mean, the food was totally yum. Totally. But it doesn't change the fact that I don't exactly like her. I mean, she's okay but I don't ever think about her. Not to mention that she looks like something that crawled out from under a rock."

Robin blinked. "You know, she's going to get her jaw fixed one day."

"It'll help."

Robin pictured the little scene Nolan Fry had

painted for her. She could hear the click of Janet's heels. She could see Janet's dark creature eyes and goony smile. She felt ashamed as if it were she, not Janet, serving Nolan a roast tenderloin lunch. And she was ashamed for feeling ashamed. "That Janet, she's a dog."

"Sad but true," Nolan said.

"You said it!"

"You like talking about your friend like this?"

"She's not my friend...and it's not because she looks like something that crawled out from under a rock, which she does, but because she's...not nice."

"*Nice!*" Nolan said. "Are you *nice*?"

"I think so. I don't know. I see what you mean." *Nice.* It was sort of a dopey, incomprehensible word. A kiss-ass word. What was so good about being *nice*?

"I'd rather be true than nice," Nolan said.

"Exactly."

"I'm true," Nolan said.

"True is good."

"Are you true?"

She closed her eyes and wondered. "I'll let you know," she whispered.

After a pause Nolan Fry said, "That seems like a true thing to say."

She turned her eyes toward his chest, where her hair sprawled across him like tentacles.

"Would it be all right if we didn't do it," Nolan

said. "Some skank in Sandy Hook gave me something nasty and my pecker's still sore." He reached lazily for his backpack and took out a prescription bottle, popped a pill, and swallowed it with cough syrup.

"I wasn't thinking we should do it," Robin said.

"You're a virgin, aren't you?"

"I'm not answering that."

"It's all right. I like virgins." They lay down again, this time with her head on his chest, and he roamed his fingers through her hair, and they were quiet for a long time. "I know exactly who you are," he whispered.

"Who?" she barely whispered back. She looked into his dozing face, so perfect even slack. She brought her cheek to his. "Who?" she whispered again.

A long while passed, or so it seemed, as she drifted in and out of sleep. "Wake me in two minutes," he murmured. "I gotta go. My mom's making Hungarian goulash for supper. Totally yum."

When two minutes seemed to have passed she took his sleeping hand and held it with both her hands. "Tell me how to be pretty, Nolan." He was in a lush, private sleep and didn't answer. She felt safe, separated from him like this, but she wanted to know all the things he seemed to know and she wanted to know how he knew them. She brought his hand to her chest and gently held it there, not ready to relinquish it. When he stirred, he raised his sleepy head and gave her a quick kiss with chapped lips.

He dropped her off at the end of her block, and she lingered for a moment. "That was fun," she said.

"Yup," Nolan said. "Thanks for smoking with me."

She stepped from the truck.

"Later," he said. Then he sped away toward his mom's Hungarian goulash.

Janet padded down the hall in Robin's direction before homeroom, dragging her feet and chewing a gob of gum. "Janet," Robin said, startled. "I've had enough of you." She left Janet standing there, baffled and peeved. Robin spent the next few days in giddy expectation as if she were gathering energy. She ate by herself in the cafeteria and darted from class to class, not unhappily, her thoughts far from Janet, who'd become remote as a star, casting only a faint light over Robin.

Days later Robin developed Nolan's cough. The cough was very dear to her and she delighted in every hack. He had given her something, like a souvenir. She decided to never speak of the Nolan episode, since once it touched the air it might disappear.

It wasn't so much that she wanted to be with Nolan, though she thought she might; rather, she wanted to be *like* him. The first time she passed him in the hall since their encounter, he lowered his eyes to her and said, "Hey you." Then most every time after he smiled, but near the end of the week it occurred to Robin that this might be the extent of her relationship with Nolan Fry.

On Friday, Janet had a note delivered to Robin while she ate a ham and cheese sandwich in the cafeteria. "At first I was furious with you, but maybe my behavior has been less than stellar lately. Please come over after school."

At the beginning of the week Robin hadn't cared if she ever spoke to Janet again, and she liked discovering what her days could feel like without Janet in them. But now she was lonely and curious and found herself walking toward her ex-friend's cantaloupe-colored house after school. In the kitchen window, she saw the back of Janet's hateful head.

"There you are," Janet said, pulling her inside. Robin felt feverish and Janet pushed her into a chair. "Are you sick? Do you need an aspirin?"

"I have a cough," Robin said, hacking several times, which made her feel better. She slid into a seat next to the watery hiss of the radiator while Janet opened a cabinet and rooted through a swarm of prescription bottles.

"I don't know where an aspirin is," Janet sighed. "There's never anything I need in this house. What you need is homemade chicken soup, but do you think we have homemade chicken soup in this house? Never. Do you think my mom ever makes homemade chicken soup? Nope. She's a bitch." She opened a can of chicken soup and placed it on the stove. Then she sat down without looking at Robin. "Frankly, you dropped me like a hot potato."

"Yes, I did."

Janet twitched in her seat. "I can probably sneak a beer. Want to split one?"

"Okay." While Janet poured the beer into glasses, Robin noticed that Janet had forgotten to light the flame under the soup. They sat together silently, drinking the beer.

"We're friends again, right?" Janet asked.

"No."

Janet folded her hands and looked solemn. "Why don't you tell me everything you can't stand about me."

"Okay."

"Wait!" Janet said, springing up from the table. "Let me get my cigarettes." She lit one and fumbled with an ashtray. "I'm ready. I feel like Anne Boleyn or something."

Robin took a sip of beer. "For starters, you're mean, Janet." Robin had lined up a few pieces of evidence and she pulled them out piece by piece, illuminating Janet's various shortcomings.

"It's just that I think it's a crying shame not to live up to your potential," Janet said, blowing a thin stream of smoke from the side of her mouth.

"I'm the kind of person who's on the quiet side. Why can't I be quiet?"

"Rightly or wrongly, I'm the kind of person who's highly opinionated."

"Well, you're ugly, Janet."

Something flashed across Janet's face, so quickly that Robin wasn't sure she had seen anything at all. "Just plain ugly," Robin said as a feeling like silk enveloped her. She took a long sip of beer, letting her eyes wander over to the window. "I'm not saying you're not a good person underneath it all, but you're a fault-finder and an extreme know-it-all."

Janet lowered her eyes and then looked up at Robin, cowed. "I guess I am at times, and I can now see how that could be extremely annoying."

"And what do you think my potential is exactly?" Robin asked.

"Well, you're very pretty for starters." Robin let Janet look deeply into her eyes. "And you have an interesting way of looking at the world. You're mostly a loyal person and you're always on time, and these things suggest a dependable person."

Robin nodded. "That's true, but that's not all I am, Janet. You're always talking so I think you miss some of my other qualities." She wondered what some of those other qualities might be. "I hope you don't think I'm being terrible or attacking you—"

Janet vigorously shook her head.

"I'm not. It's just that I have to be straight with you, Janet, because I swear sometimes you act like something that crawled out from under a rock."

Janet rose from the table. She pulled a bowl from the dishwasher and poured the soup in it. She reached to turn off the burner, saw it was off and looked confused. "Something's wrong with this soup!" she cried. She flung the pot into the sink. "My life is just retarded!" she blurted. "I hate calculus and world history. My bangs won't grow. No boys like me. I go to stupid matinées with you on Saturdays. When I need beer for a party I have to ask that pimply-community-college-moron up the street. There's nothing to look forward to ever!"

Robin assured her there were things to look forward to, and she rattled off some possibilities. "And some boys do like you—"

"Not the ones I like!"

"But still...and you're going to have your jaw fixed one day."

"Of course I am," Janet said, coolly. She turned away and started emptying the dishwasher, stacking the clean pots and pans on the counter. "What do you think my potential is, Robin?"

Robin stared at the back of Janet's head and gathered her thoughts. "You're smart. You speak extremely well. You're always able to come through with free movie tickets or wine coolers or Carvel coupons. You're a real go-getter."

"Uh-huh...I'm also savvy and enigmatic."

"Uh-huh."

Janet's face was still and soft, like a child's, when she turned to Robin. "My mom and dad left me pizza money." She picked up a twenty-dollar bill and made it dance for Robin. "Would you like to get a good dinner somewhere?" She suggested The Pier. Robin often pedaled past the chic restaurant, where the billboard said "fine dining" and featured two lobsters doing the tango. They counted the money in their wallets and decided they could afford some fine dining.

Janet went upstairs to fix her hair. Robin sat in the warm kitchen, fidgeting and feeling exhilarated. She waited a long time, mesmerized by the whir of Janet's hairdryer. Unable to keep still, she finally bounded out of her seat and wandered into the dining room, where she searched for her face in the glass doors of the breakfront. She studied her dark reflection, the curve of her cheekbone, and her long hair falling past her shoulders.

As she tried to find herself in the glass of the breakfront, she saw it. There among the plates and bowls and serving dishes was the gravy boat. It must have been the roast tenderloin lunch gravy boat. Robin took it out of the case and held it in her palm. It was very pleasing sitting on its own little plate. She turned it from side to side, admiring its ring of periwinkle flowers and its elegant curled lip. Such a fancy

thing—a gravy boat. She pictured it sitting on the
dining room table among the plates of food and linen
napkins. She imagined Nolan Fry holding it in one of
his perfect hands, the same hand that had touched
her hair, the same hand she'd held to her chest. She
saw him pouring a smooth trail of gravy over his meat
and potatoes—Nolan Fry, who would never know
what it was to be anyone but Nolan Fry.

When Janet came downstairs Robin saw she had
been crying. Janet had sprayed her hair several inch-
es off her forehead and teased it. Her eyes were
moist, but she stood on the staircase smiling brightly
and jangling her keys. "Ready?" she asked.

"Janet!" Robin said, dashing toward her. Robin
was struck hard with tangled feelings of tenderness
and guilt. She needed to gush something, to gather
up herself and Janet in some binding way. *Janet, I
didn't mean it. That's not who I am. I'm sorry, so sorry,
Janet. I like you, Janet. Janet, how pretty you look.
Janet, you are a good friend.* But she just stood there,
swelling up with the things she wanted to say, these
things that weren't true.

SAFEWAY

GEORGEANN STANDS ON THE RIM OF THE BATHTUB and peers through the little window, getting both a front and rear view of Sam Bailey's house. His dusty pickup sits next to a barrel cactus in his yard the way it always does in the late afternoon. All's quiet next door; his house is still, almost patient. "Don't be," she whispers.

As she steps down from the tub the lizard catches her eye, the same lizard she discovered a couple days ago, right after her night with Sam. While she'd brushed her teeth a movement had caught her eye and made her bend around the toilet to see the stricken lizard clinging to the bowl. "Damn," she'd said with a foamy mouth, spitting into the sink. The lizards in the kitchen crawled under the stove or refrigerator and that was the last of them, but this bathroom lizard would have to be dealt with.

And yesterday as she stepped from the shower it had darted from behind the wastebasket. "Lizard," she'd said, crouching down naked, determined to move it outside to the rocks and sun. "Go out the way you came." Two whole days in her bathroom, she thought.

Now it gazes up at her from the tiled floor. It seems paler. "What can I do?" she says. In the kitchen she spins the lazy susan and opens all the cabinets before finally grabbing a piece of rye bread and a paper bag. Back in the bathroom she waves the bread at the lizard, saying, "In the bag you go," and she places the bread in the bag with the opening facing the lizard. It hesitates with one shy foot poised in the air. "Please," Georgeann says. Three days without food or sunlight. "Eat some rye bread," she instructs the lizard, "and when I come back I'll take you outside to the yard. All right?" The little lizard arches its slender neck and then dashes behind the toilet bowl. Georgeann shakes her head and sighs.

She hurries to the car and before the air conditioner has a chance to kick in she pulls out of the driveway, watching Sam's front door as if he might suddenly appear. Yesterday, as she hung the wash, he stood in his yard cooking hot dogs while his two beagles waited by the grill, wagging their tails and looking up at Sam with a mixture of restraint and zeal. Georgeann said hello and stood with her back to him, feeling like a teenager as she emptied the washer and contemplated her underwear and bras and the grayed, stretched-out T-shirts. She rolled the wet pieces into a ball and then proceeded to hang the better-looking laundry when Sam, holding a paper plate, climbed the small fence and presented her with a hot dog in a bun, a handful of potato chips and a carrot stick.

"Oh, no thank you," she said.

"Think about it." He smiled and rested the plate on her washer.

"Really, no thanks." A fly buzzed near the hot dog and she shooed it away. "I just ate," she lied.

He shrugged and turned. "I like you," she said, intending to infer a "but," though the sentence ended cleanly, simply.

"Good." Sam climbed the fence into his yard. "I'm over here," he said, looking back at her.

Safeway is only two miles away, but Georgeann speeds along River Road with the windows wide open, and when she pulls into the parking lot she's sweaty and windblown. It takes her a moment to realize something is wrong with Safeway. The grocery store is completely dark. The automatic doors are propped open with shopping carts, and behind the darkened storefront the cashiers use flashlights to

ring up customers, who lurch through the open
doors and stare down into their bags, checking out
their purchases. Yes, they seem to be thinking, I did
get the Salisbury steak dinner and these oranges
aren't half-bad. The deli woman, a chunky woman
with a Safeway smock and a bright beehive hairdo,
stands on the curb smoking a cigarette. Georgeann
drives up and lowers the passenger window.

"Transformer blew, hon," the deli woman says.

"Can I shop?"

"Got a flashlight?"

"I think so."

The beehive shrugs and places her hands on her
wide hips. "Just be careful back by dairy. The floor is
kind of wet and you could slip and land on your ass."

Georgeann nods and swings the car into a parking space. In the trunk she finds a rusted, working
flashlight. She then joins the deli woman on the curb
and peers into the store, catching a glimpse of herself
in the chrome of the doors; she sees her Levi's and a
sleeveless denim shirt, and her silvery shoulder-length
hair tucked behind her ears. Flushed and dreamy-
looking, she looks like a person who possesses a
secret.

"Weird, huh?" beehive says, lighting another cigarette and offering the pack to Georgeann. It has
been nearly thirty years since Georgeann has had a
cigarette, but on impulse she accepts and gets light-

headed from the first drag. She takes another drag and feels the churn and sink of her bowels.

"Go on, it'll be an adventure." The beehive touches her arm; for such a stout woman her touch is delicate. The store looks inviting, cavernous. Georgeann nods and unhooks a shopping cart from the line-up.

Inside the store it is hushed and calm, except for the chug of a generator next to a checkstand. The air heavy on Georgeann's skin, and it no longer feels like a late afternoon. The cash registers make small dings and trills. Georgeann slowly pushes past the manager's specials, her flashlight illuminating piñatas—a big-mouthed fish, a mariachi, a shaggy sun and the Swiss Miss girl, who winks at Georgeann. Georgeann flashes her light in the doll's face, and the happy, braided head stares blandly back at her. She stands still and lets her eyes adjust to the low light.

In produce, water drips from the sprinklers onto the heads of lettuce and sprigs of parsley. The vegetables still look alert, almost hopeful under the beam of light. A skinny female shopper sticks a pineapple into her backpack, and Georgeann hears the zip of a zipper as the woman hurries past her with wide eyes. Georgeann, too, feels inspired to loot a little something, and she drops a ripe avocado into her purse.

"Tomatoes, corn-on-the-cob, honeydew," she says, thinking about what she needs. She is now alone among the fruits and vegetables. The arrangements seem just right under her yellow light, tomatoes next to assorted lettuces next to cucumbers next to peppers, all cousins together. She holds an eggplant, feeling its hollow bulk and wondering if she has ever really considered an eggplant—its purpleness, its prehistoric shape. She clicks off her light and stands holding the eggplant, feeling pleasantly immobile. I *love*, she thinks slowly, the words filling her head with the heaviness of sand...but what?

Georgeann tosses everything into her cart, loose and free—the perfect honeydew, several ears of corn, three rugged Idaho potatoes and a snarly turnip. She gazes into the cart, realizing this is all too much, but she can't resist tossing in two tomatoes, a peach, a plum, a nectarine, half a watermelon. The romaine smells green, a deep earthy green. She bites into an expensive yellow bell pepper, spitting a seed from the side of her mouth. The pepper tastes sweet and cool. Here in the dark she allows herself to wonder what Sam is doing. Sam's skin is bronzed and lined like the dry stream beds. He's a cabinetmaker and one-quarter Cherokee. When his dinky clothesline is full he hangs his wet laundry in the pomegranate tree. Something slithers across the loose carrots. Lizards everywhere, she thinks.

When her son Aaron was home for spring break, he and Georgeann had sat on the front stoop one night drinking margaritas. Aaron, newly in love with a freshman from Tennessee, had whispered, "Go for it, Mom," as Sam Bailey and his two beagles climbed into the pickup. Sam was tall and broad with dirty blond hair hanging into one eye. He had moved into the adobe next to hers eight weeks before, around the time the prickly pear and ocotillo went into bloom. Since then Georgeann had watched him come and go so often she had decided things about him—that he was easy to be with and spirited in a low-key way, that he was a man of his word though sulky when hurt.

Slightly tipsy, Georgeann lifted her chin as she stared at her neighbor, pretending to have noticed him for the first time. "Hell, I don't need my life turned upside down."

"Yeah?" Aaron said. "And what's so cool about right-side up?" Georgeann smiled and cupped Aaron's knee, such a large knee. He'd become a good man, she knew. Sam Bailey waved to them as he backed into the street, his beagles looking expectantly over the dash.

Georgeann moves slowly out of produce, and the pleasing stillness of fruits and vegetables, to Aisle 10: cake mixes, puddings and crusts. Not now, she thinks, leaving her cart and rounding the bend to the bread aisle.

The store has an unusual hum today, a hum like a

pulse that matches her own slow, curious heartbeat. She seems to be the only human among the bread. For a moment she feels woozy, and she squeezes a loaf of sourdough, feeling the give of soft bread. She buries her nose in the bag and sniffs the comfort of dough.

Alone in the dark with her rusted flashlight and surrounded by assorted loaves, Georgeann becomes aware of her body—its age and how long she has lived in it, the feel of blood moving through veins and the steady pump of the heart. She knows that she's going to die one day, just give out, no longer breathe and think thoughts, no longer see through these myopic eyes. She's lived in this body for nearly half a century; it is hers and hers alone. It is what she possesses.

Sam was her second lover. In the foothills under a quarter moon Georgeann had sat with him on an air mattress in the back of his pickup, sipping beer and scooping his fiery chili from a thermos. "See the Little Dipper?" he asked, leaning close and pointing into the night sky. His hand brushed her leg, and she stirred. The sky was alive with scattered stars, but she couldn't see the Little Dipper. Sam kneeled behind her and lifted her arm. "Close your left eye," he said. With her right eye Georgeann watched him trace the small, appealing ladle with their fingertips. She licked her spicy lips, figuring him to be mid-forties, maybe a little younger than she. A coyote bolted into the road and she thought, if it turns and looks my way,

I'll sleep with him. The coyote, quickly changing direction, turned its head and regarded them with bright, translucent eyes before crouching low and slinking away into the hills.

She had stretched out next to Sam, and he pressed his lips to her neck. She fingered his ear, its delicate smallness, knowing how love might get thrown into the mix and how much hurt it could bring. Later at his place they curled together like shrimp, and she held his hand close to her thumping heart. At dawn, she slipped from his bed and fled to the desert, where she sat on a large sun-washed rock and stared out at the cholla. Under the hot Tucson sun her skin heated up until the smell of Sam rose off her and enveloped her. She sat for hours, baking, feeling warm and lush, until finally she returned home.

Georgeann holds English muffins and nine-grain, giving each bag a squeeze but unable to choose. Clutching both bags, she searches for her cart. In front of the Crackerjack display sits a cart holding Muenster cheese, cherries, and bubble bath. Bubbles, she thinks longingly. The cart has the look of abandonment, and Georgeann wheels off with it. There will be many other days for vegetables, she decides.

Up ahead a small boy sits in a cart, singing a song about a boy and a girl in a canoe while his mother bends near a low shelf. Georgeann stares at the child and listens. His voice is high and tuneless. She can't see the boy's eyes, just the darkness of his sockets. As Georgeann comes up next to the child he doesn't stop singing, only hesitates for a second, and then continues while Georgeann runs her hand over his downy head. He tips his face up toward her. He's silky-headed and earnest, his hair so fine between her fingers she would like to lean down and sniff him.

Georgeann had a husband for many years and together they'd made a baby, who has probably turned to dust in the cemetery up in the foothills by now. The baby had been perfect but blue and he wouldn't breathe. Her baby with his perfect head, heavy with skull and brains, lay curled and lifeless in her arms. The doctors only let her and Ross visit with the little boy for a few moments. Even chimpanzees are more civilized; they carry around their dead for days.

The death of their baby unlinked Georgeann and Ross from each other. They turned their backs, lowered their eyes and erased their faces, but they went on folding the towels, unclogging the bathroom drain, watering the fish pond, ordering Chinese, playing Rummy.

Then when they adopted Aaron and he came to them at two years old with a bad haircut and a clear, steady gaze they were linked together again by the urgency to show him things. They took trips by car and trips by plane to the Grand Canyon, Disneyland, the meteor crater, the petrified forest. Georgeann taught him how to do the twist and make a potato chip sandwich. Ross taught him how to care for a goldfish and stand on his hands. Lit with glee, they lived like Spaniards, eating charred pork chops at eleven p.m., tired and flushed, with sleepy Aaron munching, his lids half-closed, his body ready to topple over. "Get the chop out of your ear, sweetie," Georgeann had said. She and Ross were deliriously in love with him, but his arrival didn't do a damn thing about the hollow pit opened up in her by the dead baby. The center of her pain had been scooped out, but the air left there was dry and brittle.

Georgeann quickly drops her hand from the boy's head and pushes her cart along as the mother moves toward her son. Up ahead a small woman leans against the frozen foods, holding a lit candle. "I picked this up in housewares," she says.

"Good thinking."

"My boyfriend's got the flashlight in the potato chip aisle. I snuck away." She runs her fingers through the air. Her shopping cart holds cereal and yams.

Georgeann clicks off her flashlight and leans over the freezer, expecting frosty air but the air is still and watery. She holds a package of asparagus to her forehead and sighs, feeling the coolness.

"I could kill him," the woman murmurs.

"Who?"

"My boyfriend."

"What did he do?" Georgeann whispers.

"He's got some side action going on," the woman whispers back.

"Your boyfriend?"

"My boyfriend."

"Dump him," Georgeann says.

"I should, shouldn't I?"

Georgeann can tell that the woman probably won't, that she'll hold on to him for longer than she should, and Georgeann has the urge to slap her. "Really, you should," she says instead, touching the woman's thin arm.

"I know!" the woman says. "I know!"

Georgeann nods.

A gangly man moves along the meat counter, rustling through a bag and crunching.

"That's him," the woman says.

The man's crunch suddenly infuriates Georgeann. How dare this cheater crunch so delicately, so innocuously! Georgeann reaches for a yam from the woman's cart and hurls it through the air, striking the cruncher on the back of the head. Oh, the hearty smack! "Shit!" he yells, quickly moving away. Georgeann throws another yam and so does the woman, but they miss and hit the meat counter instead. They gather up more yams, hugging them to their chests, and run after the strange man. They throw yams in his direction until he outruns them, disappearing down the household cleaner aisle.

"I'm not sure that was him," the woman says.

"That must have been him!"

Just last week Georgeann ran into Ross outside of Target. I spent twenty-three years with you, Georgeann thought, looking at his head of sparse hair, which had gone crinkly like dried seaweed and turned the color of ash. In his arms he held his daughter, a tiny blonde girl with flyaway hair. Ross married the woman he'd been running around with the last couple years of their marriage, a younger woman with long gauze skirts and cool blue eyes, who left a whiff of patchouli in her wake.

Outside Target, as his tiny daughter twisted and jumped in his arms, wanting to ride the fifty-cent Dumbo, Georgeann waved to him. Three years later she was able to do that. He lifted his arm, smiled widely and walked toward her, but she moved swiftly through the double doors without a backward glance.

Georgeann had known in her heart before she knew in her head that Ross was cheating on her. When she'd found him throwing pennies in the garbage, sweeping them off his dresser into the trash bag, she asked herself, just who is he—this careless, careless man? Then without conscious effort her love began to untangle its hold and dissolve.

"Listen to me," Georgeann now says to the woman, grabbing her arm. "Listen…" But she doesn't know what to say to her; Georgeann's own experiences have left deep impressions, but where, she wonders, is the grace of wisdom? "Come," she says instead, following the scent of chocolate and butter as she steers the woman to the bakery counter at the back of the store. The candle casts a warm, inviting glow on the trays of round butter cookies sparkling with sugar, little buttery men filled with chocolate and raspberry, cupcakes dipped in rainbow sprinkles, a small cake decorated with a chocolate ribbon. "Here," she says, pulling the woman behind the counter.

The sweets are gleaming and beautiful, and at this moment everything feels possible to Georgeann—the world feels vast and comforting. Clarity pushes in on her amid the scent of luscious chocolate. Move it, it tells her; *move, move.* They kneel in front of the goodies. "Eat!" Georgeann cries, sliding open the glass case. "Eat something."

Slowly they reach into the case and eat one cookie at a time. Soon they start exchanging treats, passing the fanciest and the gooiest ones to each other. Georgeann wants to eat everything. She grabs an éclair, licks the icing and then stuffs it in her mouth. The woman's hand hovers over a tray, unable to decide. Her hand creeps back to her side and thrusts forward, snatching a cupcake and stuffing it, paper and all, into her mouth. Georgeann eats a cannoli, feeling crumbs fall from her lips onto her lap.

The woman and Georgeann have chocolate rings around their mouths. Georgeann wipes her own mouth, feeling queasy with sticky sweetness, but she's tempted by a thick brownie. It's heavy and slick with icing, and she swallows it down in gobs. Gooey chocolate coats the roof of her mouth. As she stuffs in the rest of the brownie she feels her bowels turn. "I have to find a bathroom," she says, standing and bumping into the cookie case.

The woman makes a small, understanding noise as Georgeann rushes to the rear corner of the store, where a light shines. A stockboy mops the floor by the dairy case, his large flashlight illuminating a milky puddle. "The bathroom," Georgeann says. "Where is it?"

"The bathroom isn't for customers, lady," he says, turning from her and going over her wet footprints with the mop.

"I have to go!" She clutches his arm; it is a skinny boy's arm.

He makes a sour, huffy noise that says, just who do you think you are? I haven't a clue, kiddo, she thinks. He leads the way through a set of metal doors and into the meat locker where hunks of beef hang from hooks. "You should have gone before you came here."

"Hurry," she says, pulling him along faster. She's not sure she will make it.

He shines his light into the dirty little bathroom so she gets an idea where the toilet is, before he gives her a small push and shuts her in.

Georgeann unbuckles her jeans. Constipation is more her style, but now she has to take an urgent shit in the blackness of Safeway. The air is cold and creepy on her naked skin as she squats over the toilet until she must sit. Feeling along the wall she finds the roll of toilet paper.

There must be a mirror above the sink, and she reaches out and touches the smooth, chilly surface, but in the darkness there is no reassurance of her face. She is just a woman alone in a dank bathroom, a woman who wishes she'd lived a little better. At this moment she's certain a touch of rot has taken root inside her heart, where instead there might have been expansion. She also knows she still might live better if she knew how not to be afraid. Her heart pounds loudly, letting her know she is still very much alive, as she gropes with the faucet and feels for the soap dispenser. When she flushes she hopes it all goes down.

There is no stockboy with a flashlight waiting for her when she opens the door. The overhead lights begin to flicker as she makes her way past the slabs of bloody meat. It is a hard life, there's no doubt. She gives the side of a cow a fairly good punch. It is a cold and dignified piece of beast. Large and stupid and ugly, but it is what it is.

On the other side of the double doors, the lights continue to flicker in spurts, and Georgeann moves quickly to the front of the store, ready to leave. By the checkout line she eyes a shopping cart wedged against the magazine rack holding a T-bone steak and a five-pound bag of potatoes. "Is this anybody's?" Georgeann asks.

The checkout girl shrugs under the sputtering lights. Georgeann lifts the food onto the conveyer belt and digs for her wallet, discovering the avocado, ripe and warm, buried in her purse. After she pays the girl she carries her bag to the car, squinting into the brightness. The sunset is a swirl of red and purple melting together and hanging low over the Tucson Mountains.

When Georgeann returns home she peers under the living room curtains at Sam Bailey's salmon-colored adobe, listening to the whir of his swamp cooler, watching the billow of his ratty T-shirts on the clothesline. "You," she says; the word sounds almost accusatory.

She takes a cool bath. The rye bread is stale without any nibbles in it and there is no sign of the lizard—hopefully it found its way out to the yard, she thinks, biting into the hard bread and feeling the pressure between her teeth. She changes into her nightgown and moves to the living room, feeling deeply unsatisfied, and sits in different chairs, finally falling to sleep on the couch.

At dawn, sunlight fills the room and she wanders into the bathroom, where she discovers the lizard clinging to the side of the bathtub. "Oh!" she yells, kneeling in front of it. "You're going to die on me, aren't you?" The lizard is completely still and she notes the translucent front legs, as elegant as a dancer's, and the dainty tip of its tail. "Lovely," she whispers. She gently touches it with one finger. "Please," she whispers, her voice faint and airy. "I won't hurt you." The lizard turns its neck and looks into her eyes with its own black, unreadable ones. It is weak, she can see. Its body has probably started in on the business of dying. "Let me take you outside," she whispers. She brushes it into her hand and feels the little body there in her palm, trusting her, and she wonders at the mystery of this.

Warmth rises from the earth, this desert valley, beneath her bare feet as she moves slowly past the cholla and rose bushes. Cupping her hands, she talks to the lizard in a low, soothing voice and sets it down next to the Joshua tree. "Be well," she says as the lizard moves uncertainly across her fingers to the ground.

As she stands, she sees Sam Bailey sitting on his

back stoop, working his feet into a pair of socks. One of his beagles stretches out next to him. Faint music is playing on a transistor radio. Sam sees her then, half-hidden by the Joshua tree, standing in her night-gown. A warm breeze, like a breath emptying from the lungs, blows through her yard into his as she moves toward him.

WILDLIFE OF AMERICA

MY SISTER FRANKIE'S EVENING-OF-BEAUTY COUPON was good only on Fridays, so she'd made an appointment for this coming one when she'd spend the evening swaddled in seaweed and dipped in Middle Eastern mud, and since my brother-in-law Chuck had his impotence support group, after which he and the guys would usually go for a beer, could I please babysit?

I had left my life in New York City and for the past month had been rehabilitating in New Jersey in the half-finished apartment over Frankie's garage. Our deal was that I'd babysit my niece and nephew on occasion, though it hadn't quite worked out yet. Frankie stood at the bottom of the stairs to the apartment, balancing a load of laundry on her hip, waiting for my answer. We had the same mass of dark curly hair and we were both slightly pear-shaped with pitted cheeks from long-ago acne.

"Sorry, Frankie," I said. "But I have a date."

Slowly, she made a face at me. "Shit on a stick! I'm going to get stuck with Constance Poblanski. Fiona, how much do you want to bet I'm going to get stuck with Constance Poblanski?"

"You're going to get stuck with Constance Poblanski," I said.

Frankie sighed.

"Shit on a stick," I said, sympathetically.

"Well, I hope you get laid," she said.

"Thank you."

Yesterday, after the stickup at Wawa where I met Derek Head, Frankie and I had sat at her kitchen table, eating fat-free cream cheese on rice cakes, as I described in great detail Derek Head's looks, exactly what words passed between us, how I felt talking with him, how I thought he felt, what I thought could happen between us, what I thought the children we would never have might look like, with his hypnotic avocado eyes and all.

"I'm doing darks, got any?" Frankie said, putting down the laundry basket.

I went for a pair of jeans and some shirts, and as I came back to the top of the stairs, she was reaching under her T-shirt and unhooking her bra. She slid one strap off one arm, then the other, and with a fast pull—like a magician—whipped free a zebra-striped padded push-up number and dropped it into the basket. She had a Frederick's of Hollywood charge account and loved ultra-fancy and lewd underwear— bras that pushed them up and hauled them out or bras that left nothing to the imagination—but over this stuff she wore the jeans, T-shirts and cardigan sweaters of every other good suburban citizen. Frankie wasn't happy. I wasn't happy. I loved her more than anyone at the moment. Her sadness was so terrible and tender.

I aimed for the basket and my clothes hit the top of the heap. "Next time I will absolutely babysit," I told her.

"I look forward to it," she said, picking up the load. "'Cause," she said, shaking a finger at me, "I'm going to get stuck with Constance Poblanski."

Chuck was making spaghetti with garlic, olive oil, and red pepper, and the smell wafted over the garage, drawing me out of my apartment even though I had just taken a long bath and was still shriveled. With wet hair dripping down my shirt, I entered the kitchen where Frankie was on the phone, rolling her eyes to the ceiling. "So, we'll see you at six on Friday. Don't be late." Frankie forced a laughed and hung up. "Guess who we got?" she said in a low, injured voice.

Chuck had just come home from his shift and still wore his police uniform, though he had unbuttoned the shirt. He was muscular and Italian and on the short side, and he stood over the sizzling frying pan. "Don't get all worked up, Frank," he said.

"I enjoy getting worked up," she said, hotly.

"I enjoy watching you enjoy getting worked up," I said and smiled. I took Chuck's spoon and had a little taste.

"Two cuckoo birds," Chuck said, flashing us a smile.

My sister could only ever get the lackluster Constance Poblanski to babysit when she wanted the sweet and radiant Laura Rossi. Frankie would always call Laura first, but Laura, without fail, would already be booked with the Andersons. Both girls lived in the neighborhood and were headed to Rutgers in the fall, and they seemed to be great friends, which was incomprehensible to Frankie. Laura Rossi had a bright, nervous energy while Constance Poblanski burned at a lower wattage, raising her plucked brows and flaring those elegant nostrils in a vague scorn. Laura was a nailbiter, her only beauty aids a dab of lip gloss and a plastic barrette. She had, we all agreed, an astonishing smile. God had been equally kind to Constance, though Constance fooled with Mother Nature, yanking and spraying that mass of hair to unnatural heights and streaking it an orangey-blonde.

But Constance wasn't the issue here. The issue was the Andersons—Lord and Lady Anderson, as Frankie called them—who were able to get the good babysitter. Frankie saw the whole situation as the inequitable universe dispensing the fair and virtuous Laura to the fair and virtuous Andersons, while she got stuck with Constance.

Frankie had had this petty but debilitating obsession with the Andersons for as long as they'd been her neighbors. It seemed to Frankie that the Lord and Lady were everything she and Chuck weren't. The Andersons had money, but more importantly they acted as though they had the secret knowledge that abundance would always be their lot. Their rhododendron had grown to the size of an African elephant and bloomed flowers the size of your head. They had an interior designer who dabbled in feng shui and made sure that any bad energy that got dumped in their living room would be swept right out the front door and wouldn't spill into their hallways and soak into their walls. They had their house professionally painted an enticing mix of beiges and browns that made me think of cake mix and icing. Frankie and Chuck had gotten on ladders and slopped their own house a color resembling French's mustard. *Well, it didn't look that way in the can.* They couldn't quite afford the neighborhood but Frankie had insisted they try. Chuck was not infected with

Anderson obsession. He was a shy, easygoing cop who loved his wife and wanted to please her. Their house was big and old and weather-beaten. With its sagging gutters it wore a frown similar to Frankie's.

Lord Anderson was a young, stocky rheumatologist with close-clipped hair, resembling his manicured lawn. He had a kindly, long face with a full-bodied nose and a habit of standing with his hands on his hips. In the warm months he liked to pull out the garden hose and wash and wax his Infiniti. Lady Anderson had girlishly shiny hair and freckled skin. She didn't wear makeup and her teeth were a bit jumbled, but she had glamorous bones. They often strolled the block hand in hand, their daughter Dana, the heiress, trailing them on her bike, pink and white streamers dangling from the handlebars.

As luck would have it, the heiress and my niece Melody were in the same class in the same private school, which my sister and brother-in-law couldn't really afford. During Dental Awareness week, Melody had been cast as a cavity in a skit on personal hygiene while the Heiress Anderson got to charge in with a large paper toothbrush saving the day. "Why does that kid get to be the savior while mine gets to rot?" Frankie later yelled. It didn't matter to Frankie that Melody was a perfect cavity. I knew this because I sat with Frankie in the audience, watching the impish and wiry Melody do her decay dance.

"Some people just seem to live charmed lives," Frankie said, shaking her head. I had to say, now that I was living with Frankie and Chuck, I enjoyed the Anderson obsession. I liked hearing tale after tale about the Lord and Lady. This preoccupation kept me from my own thoughts.

We sat down to eat, and Chuck herded the kids to the table and tied a dishtowel around Marcus's neck. "You guys like Constance Poblanski?" Chuck asked.

"She lets us watch naked butts," Marcus said, forking up one strand of spaghetti.

"Not real live naked butts," Melody said. "Baboon butts. The Discovery Channel."

"Still," Marcus said, cocking his head to the side.

"A naked butt's a naked butt," Chuck said, winking. Frankie smiled. She and Chuck had been together for almost eighteen years. They met in a human sexuality class at the community college, where as an icebreaker on the first day the teacher asked the students to come up with slang terms for genitalia. When they were doing female genitals the guy Frankie had been dating volunteered, "bearded clam." Romantically, it was over for her after that. Chuck squirmed and blushed when he was called on and finally whispered, "pussy." Frankie, too, could barely get out "wang."

My boyfriend Dean and I had been going out for two years, and I wasn't sure where we were headed, but the relationship was as comfortable as slippers. I lived on Cherry Lane in Greenwich Village, Dean lived in Tribeca. We spent lots of time together with our friends, drinking beer and eating hamburgers at the Ear Inn like all of us were twenty-four instead of thirty-four. I knew I probably should have been thinking of the future. Was this relationship moving forward or had we stalled out? Did I want to get married? I thought I did. Then last fall when the leaves started to turn beautiful and crisp, Dean and my good friend Patty came over to my place, pale and somber, and told me they had something very difficult to say. I'd been defrosting my freezer, which was like the Arctic. I had bowls of hot water in there to speed up the job. I was wearing sweats and socks when they told me they'd fallen in love. They were quick to point out that they hadn't acted on it, that they'd only spoken about what was to be done, that at this point their relationship just involved words and feelings. My stomach did a flip, and I lowered myself right to the floor. I wanted to yell but found I had no voice. "Why didn't you just screw each other and shut the hell up," I whispered. "You think it's easier on me that you love each other minus the screwing?"

"We were thinking of you, Fiona."

"We love you, Fiona."

"If you think this isn't hard on us, Fiona, you're mistaken."

I couldn't remember who said what; they seemed to be interlinked, two bodies sharing the same mind. I had an out-of-body experience. I felt myself calmly leave the premises of my body and rise to the ceiling and remain stuck there against the paint chips. *We* and *us*, they said; *Fiona*, they said over and over. I was no longer part of the equation. In the kitchen, chunks of ice splintered and crashed in the freezer. I thought I'd crack in two.

I either slept twelve to fourteen hours a night or couldn't keep still. I couldn't bear to be in my apartment on Cherry Lane. I couldn't bear to sleep in my bed. I wrestled with the ancient two-ton sofa bed in my living room and finally managed to open it, but it had a powerful defective spring and sprang shut like a venus flytrap, capturing me in the mattress. I shimmied out, but every muscle in my body hurt for days. I called in sick to work and bought stacks of magazines. I limped to Washington Square Park, furiously flipping pages but unable to concentrate. A pigeon flew up into my face, and I swatted it in the head with a copy of *The Economist*. I railed at Patty and Dean late at night, alone in my apartment. I handled the whole thing terribly; of course, terrible was my only option. Initially, I had our friends' sympathy but after a while I lost their company. Around the holidays a few friends told me I was a drag to be around. They told me I had to get over it already. "Easy for you to say," I spewed, feeling my words roil with something rank and foamy. "No one's saying it's easy," they'd counter. Couldn't they see I'd been thrown to the ground and didn't know how to get up? And through it all Dean and Patty remained together, sharing their *words* and *feelings*, and presumably screwing, too.

By March I was teeming with vile thoughts and rage, probably trailing a slime residue. My boss, the remarkable Mr. Snodgrass, had called me into his office and shut the door. "Look, Fiona," he said. "I'm gonna finagle disability for you. I'll send you to a doctor friend of mine and you'll take some time off, work this through." I didn't want free time on my hands, even though I'd come to loathe my job in member services at Wildlife of America. I once loved the work, but these past few months I'd lost my zest and found myself getting snarly with the members. "I'm going to report you," said a Doris Pitts, a twenty-year member, when I told her I didn't care if she was a twenty-minute member. "Wait your turn, Laverne," was how I put it.

It had all gone down so easily. I saw the doctor, the paperwork was filled out; I sublet my place on Cherry Lane, packed up some boxes, and within a week moved to Frankie and Chuck's in Little Silver,

New Jersey. When I'd called Frankie I wept so hard I could barely speak. "Those bastards, those double-crossers, those fuckers," she said. At first I thought she meant Dean and Patty, but then realized she was lumping together all the bastards, double-crossers and fuckers we'd ever known. She sighed and said, "You just don't know who you'll fall in love with." This made me cry harder. "You come here," she said. "Live in the apartment." "I love you," she yelled over my tears. "I love you back," I yelled. We yelled about many things, especially all the things we cherished and despised, working ourselves up until we were both ecstatic and exhausted.

Coming to New Jersey was like taking a bath. At least I felt clean. I rode a bike every day and did crosswords. I drank tea at the Local Drip and met a few local drips. Little Silver, I discovered, actually had a five-and-dime called Five & Dime. I loved to cruise the dusty aisles, examining the junk crammed on the shelves in wobbly heaps. I'd buy my nephew and niece some tchotchkes: yo-yos, some glitter and glue. I'd buy myself glow-in-the-dark stars, a plastic cigarette holder, plastic daisy flip-flops, a Magilla Gorilla wall clock, conch shells, magenta nail polish, seahorse erasers, corn-on-the-cob refrigerator magnets. I borrowed the Babcocks' mutt and walked the beach, wearing a windbreaker and the daisy flip-flops. I liked lifting my face to the sun. Every week I cashed my disability check and carried around hundreds of dollars; I didn't have many places to spend it since Frankie and Chuck wouldn't take any money from me. I'd flip through Frankie's recipe books and make menu decisions and then bike over to the Grand Union and buy egg noodles and butter and cream and various cuts of beef and chicken, and I'd make us beef stroganoff and meatloaf and mashed potatoes, honey mustard chicken and roasted potatoes. I played Barbershop Play-Doh with my niece and nephew. I'd send the blue dough spouting through the holes on the plastic figures' heads and then I'd give them chic haircuts with the plastic scissors. When Chuck worked nights, Frankie pulled out moldy-smelling games she'd saved from when we were teenagers. We drank Bloody Marys and ate tortilla chips and I'd wear my Five & Dime tiara as we played Mystery Date, hoping not to open the door on Poindexter.

The next night I made stuffed cabbage, and after dinner Chuck washed the dishes and the kids dried them. Frankie was still in her white X-ray technician uniform and white clogs as she peered out from behind the living room curtain. Lord Anderson stood on his lawn, one hand on his hip, the other holding a cell phone to his ear as he made a wide circle on the grass. The sun was setting and gave the neighborhood a warm glow.

"Just look at him," Frankie said.

"And?" I said.

"I bet he can get it up," she whispered to me. "I bet he does the Lady just fine."

The Lord bobbed his head in elaborate nods, as in: *Of course, just fine, sure buddy, you bet.* "Yes, yes, yes," Frankie said. "The magic word at the palace."

"Frankie, he's kind of an ordinary guy, if you ask me."

She snickered. "He's gonna get grass stains," she said, referring to his socks. Then, as if on cue, Lady Anderson appeared on the steps holding his sneakers. "See, she intuits his every need," Frankie said. The Lord turned and gave his wife a wave and continued nodding his ordinary head. Lady Anderson threw one of his sneakers and it landed next to him, and as she tossed the other he moved in her direction and got clocked on the ear.

"Huh!" I said, elbowing Frankie, who almost looked disappointed.

Frankie was convinced that the Andersons always did the right thing. Once when the town had wanted to open the dead end at the end of their development to make an alternate route for traffic, the Andersons held a block meeting in their creamy home and served wine and brie while they outlined a plan of action against the proposal. Frankie believed because their lives were blessed they could afford such generosity. My sister had once held a block meeting herself. She stood on her crumbling stoop handing out flyers while snow fell from the clouds. I remembered this; I took the train from New York to spend the day with her, and I wound up watching her through the window from my seat on the couch as she yelled about zoning ordinances, her teeth chattering. "Why didn't you invite them in?" I later asked. "The house's a mess." But her house was always a mess, and at least people would have been warm. "*Who* would invite the whole block in?" she asked. Well, a year later the Andersons would, and it was just another blow to my sister, proving that she would never have membership in that elite league to which the Andersons belonged.

A couple days before I had stopped in Wawa for an ice pop. I was standing over the freezer, debating between orange and piña colada when this flirty guy swooped in next to me and reached for a toasted almond bar. As we both stood in line at the counter, the guy in front of me pulled out a gun and aimed it at the young slack-jawed clerk. "Keep it quiet. Open the drawer. Empty the bills," he said.

The clerk did just that, handing a short stack of bills to the thief, who thrust them into his pocket. "Everybody," the thief said as he reached the door,

"Hands where I can see them, hands where I can see them." I held my ice pop in the air and so did the guy behind me. "Count to sixty," he instructed us as he darted through the door and into the sunshine.

"That S.O.B.," the flirty guy said. The clerk was mouthing: three, four, five. "Where's the alarm?" the flirt asked, taking charge and unpeeling his toasted almond bar. "We have to stay, we're witnesses," he said to me with a smile, as if being held up in Wawa was a regular occurrence for him, and he extended his hand and introduced himself as Derek Head.

My brother-in-law Chuck was the first on the scene, weighted down and jingly with the crackly radio, the billy club, the handcuffs, the gun and the holster. "Hey, look who it is," he said, coming up beside me. "Causing trouble?"

"Just a regular stickup in suburbia," I said.

Chuck and his partner took down our accounts, but when they wanted a physical description I was at a loss.

"He had a blockish head, don't you think?" Derek Head said.

"Mmmm," I said. Somehow staring at the gunman didn't seem to be the right etiquette, and then I had spotted the Toblerone bar in front of me and was thinking that under the circumstances, which seemed like life or death ones, there was no reason I shouldn't indulge my urge. I hardly noticed the guy.

While we talked, I returned my ice pop to the freezer and reached for the Toblerone, opening its nifty box and beginning to eat the luscious chocolate. "The guy sounded irritated," I volunteered. "Like maybe he was ready for a new line of work." Derek Head and I laughed. He had a wet mouth and shiny teeth and was pretty handsome, even with vanilla ice cream dotted on his chin. Chuck watched me tolerantly, his radio emitting small squawks.

We rode in the back seat of Chuck's squad car—neither of us having paid for our purchases, I'd realized—to look at pictures at the station house. As Derek talked to me, he touched my hand, my arm. Chuck was enjoying this, looking from me to Derek Head in the rearview mirror.

I didn't think I'd be much help, so I ate the chocolate while my eyes glazed over page after page of assorted criminals. When Derek Head cried, "Here's the little weasel," I had to admit he was right; it was as if my brain had filed him away in some lower chamber and when the trigger came he was released back into memory. The guy was young and friendly-looking, and his mug shot easily could have been a yearbook photo. His previous arrests were for petty larceny, breaking and entering.

When Derek Head got ready to leave, he leaned in close to me and asked for my number. I scribbled away, as happy as a lark while Chuck pretended to shuffle papers. When Derek left, Chuck let loose a laugh. "You like old lizard eyes?"

"I'd call them bedroom eyes. You know him?"

"Nope," Chuck said, "But I'm gonna check him out." A snapshot of Frankie was pinned to the bulletin board next to Chuck's desk. She was squinting in the sun, her face hopeful and blameless and ten years younger. She wore, I realized, a similar expression to the gunman. I placed her photo next to his.

"Malcontent," I said, making up her crime. I waited for Chuck to smile.

Chuck watched me. "Fiona, does Frankie like me?"

I tacked the photo back to the board and looked at him.

"I know she loves me..." he said.

On Friday, I took two hours getting ready for my date—showering, air-drying, and dancing naked to the Eurythmics, "Sisters Are Doin' It for Themselves." The kids banged on my door, and I shooed them away. I was looking forward to a whiskey sour and a little action, and I felt my body temperature rise. I had hung posters of flowers and bees and vines over the silvery insulation, but the apartment still looked crappy and messy, and everything that belonged in a drawer, on a hanger, or on a shelf, I threw into the cockeyed closet. I hoped we could go to his place, but then again you could never foresee what the evening would bring.

I went downstairs in my robe, and as I came up the back steps of the house, I heard Frankie say, "Fiona wants to get laid."

She and Chuck seemed to be murmuring sympathetically when I stepped through the back door. "What time is he picking you up?" Frankie asked.

"He's not. I'm meeting him at the Chowder Pot." Frankie and Chuck shared a look. They had the same ideas about mating rituals—the male is supposed to pick up the female in his swanky car.

"Bring a credit card, Fiona, or plan on washing dishes," Chuck said.

"Oh, come on," I said. "Did you get anything on him anyway?"

"Old bedroom eyes has a couple misdemeanors. Minor traffic violations. Lewd conduct, way back."

"Have Fiona tailed," Frankie suggested. "What if this character drags her into the woods and puts her in a pot?"

"Nah, Fiona wouldn't make good soup." He smiled.

"I didn't realize living in suburbia could be such an adventure," I said. What could Derek Head have done? Pissed in public?

"This is as good as it gets." Frankie removed her eye makeup with a tissue. "I'm going to have my top layer of epidermis sanded off, and did you know all this dipping, sanding and steaming takes four and a half hours?" she said, reading off a brochure from the salon. "I'll be as smooth and as sleek as a seal."

"I look forward to it," Chuck said. "You need money, Fiona?" He dug through his wallet.

"Give her fifty," Frankie said.

"Listen to you two!" I said. "I'm fine, I'm *fine*."

A horn tooted out front. "That's my ride. A good evening, all," Chuck said, planting a kiss on Frankie's head. I wondered if the support group chatter was all penis-based and I wondered what Frankie knew about it, but she looked almost pleased reading her brochure so I left her in peace and went up to the apartment to get changed.

When I was leaving for my date, Constance Poblanski was perched on Frankie's couch, and Melody and Marcus were in their shorty pajamas, slumped over the recliner. "Hey," I said, walking through the living room. Constance grunted hello. She had one of those plastic see-through purses, and I could see all her stuff. She had little pots and tubes and wands of makeup, a copy of *Sense and Sensibility*, some dollar bills and coins, a super tampon, and a packet of birth control pills, missing its lid. I could see that she had five of the white pills left before she'd take the brown ones; five days until her period, hence the super tampon. Constance

Poblanski was a girl prepared.

"Is babysitting cramping your style, Constance?"
I said in a friendly way.

"Con, I go by Con," she said, running her fingers
through that hill of hair. She narrowed her eyes. "My
mom's got that dress."

The thought of the squat and mustached pierogie-
making Mrs. Poblanski in my little sundress, pur-
chased with one of Frankie's coupons, brought an
uninspiring picture to mind. "*Con*, don't flush your
super tampon or you'll be in for a super mess. The toilet backs up." I made a sad face and waved goodbye.

The kids followed me to the door. "I hope he's
not a dork-a-matic," Melody said, pressing her nose
up against the screen.

"Thank you, honey."

As I rode my bike the setting sun cast shades of
pink and purple across the sky. It was a mild April
evening and my flouncy sundress didn't interfere
with pedaling. I might never return to New York, I
decided. I might stay here in the Garden State forever. Cars passed me silently and fresh air blew across
the sea.

I locked up my bike and walked into the noisy
Chowder Pot, where the tables were packed and a
small, ornery crowd waited by the hostess station. I
spotted Derek Head at the bar, drinking a martini,

and he spotted me too and moseyed over. "I've been waiting," he said, giving me a squeeze.

"Here I am." I smiled. He smiled back, half-lit.

"Come on, I've got a table reserved."

Now I was impressed. We weaved through the crowded room, to the cut-off by the bathrooms, where there was a staircase I'd never noticed before blocked off with a velvet rope.

"After you," he said, lifting the rope. I climbed the stairs, wondering what could be on the second floor of the Chowder Pot. We walked through a wall of beads into a smoky dark room with couches, end tables, fringy lamps, and smooching couples, like an orgy room. I looked at Derek Head and he smiled. "Never been up here?" I shook my head. He led me over to a couch with a reserved sign. He chucked the sign to the other end of the couch and grabbed me and gave me a hearty kiss. I laughed out loud, shaking my head at all of this. In seconds the owner of the Chowder Pot, a Seymour with a last name that sounded like soufflé, whose picture I'd often seen in *The Little Silver Herald* for sponsoring the Polar Bear Club's annual April swim or judging the Easter egg hunt, took our drink order. I relaxed into the deep comfy couch. The music was smooth and bluesy, and everyone in the room shined. Derek Head held my hand.

"Is this room a secret?" I felt certain Frankie didn't know about it.

"Some secret," he said, waving his hand around the room. "Let's get lots of appetizers. I'm an appetizers man."

We ordered fried calamari, a stuffed artichoke, clams casino, and a shrimp cocktail from Seymour Soufflé. Derek Head and I slurped our drinks and kissed. Every time I put down my whiskey sour it seemed to refill itself. I spotted Lord and Lady Anderson several couches away, kissing, the Lord's hands cupping the Lady's glossy head. I was mildly buzzed, a pleasant hum moving through my blood. The food came, piles of it, and we spread it around the top of a small chest of drawers and dug in. In between bites and sips, we'd kiss some more. Derek Head took a bite of shrimp, nibbled on my neck, then placed the half-bitten shrimp into my mouth. He'd wait for me to finish chewing and then French kiss me. I was having, I decided, the greatest time of my life, which made me like Derek Head.

"What's your story, Fiona? You got a boyfriend?"

"Well, no." He smiled, and I realized either way was all right with him.

We were working on the stuffed artichoke when he said, "My sweetheart gave me the old heave-ho." I realized I didn't care as I scraped a leaf against my teeth.

"Are you sad?" I asked, for something to say.

"Knife," he said, stabbing himself in the heart

with a clamshell.

"A good friend of mine and my boyfriend fell in love with each other." I wanted to shut him up and get back to the kissing. I didn't want the appetizers to ever end. Derek Head dipped a piece of squid in cocktail sauce and fed me.

"Well, that'll take the stars out of your eyes." He looked into my eyes to see the state of the little universes. I batted them, wondering how I was progressing. I still wasn't sure. We were making out again, this time falling sideways onto the couch while Seymour Soufflé cleared away our dishes.

After a time, Derek Head brushed hair from my forehead and said, "Let's go to your place."

"Can we go to yours?"

"This is mine," he said. "This is my bed." When I looked doubtful, he took a key from his jeans and opened a padlock on the chest of drawers, pulling out a pillow and a pair of boxer shorts. "This is the state of affairs after the old heave-ho."

We ordered a drink for the road, smooching the whole while. Then Derek Head put the reserved sign back on his chest of drawers. "I don't want anyone on my bed while I'm gone, you see." Seymour Soufflé nodded to us as we left.

I was happy and tipsy. "Where are you parked?" I asked.

"Baby, my vehicle is impounded like my heart,"

he said, growing drunker in the cool air and sounding like a bad Southern novelist. "Where might yours be?"

I led him over to my bike and wiggled my own key in front of his face. Derek Head pedaled while I sat on the handlebars, and we weaved down the dimly lit streets as he sang a few verses of "God Bless America."

We rode into Frankie's development. The sycamores seemed welcoming and suburbia such a civil place. Derek Head dropped me off on Frankie and Chuck's lawn and then proceeded to pop a few wheelies in the street. I peered in the living room window, but there was no Con in sight. I crept along the side of the house and saw her standing in Frankie and Chuck's bedroom, trying on Frankie's fancy bras, twirling in front of the mirror, admiring herself. *What to do, what to do*? I couldn't think. Wear the underpants of a good citizen and you won't have these problems.

Derek Head had fallen off the bicycle and skinned his knee. He came hobbling over, and I yanked him around back and up the stairs to my Five & Dime decorated apartment. We fell onto the little bed, but some of the magic was gone. We reeked of alcohol. Before long we were back in the groove, and the very drunk Derek Head had no problem getting it up and keeping it up. We went at it, and several minutes later we were done. Now that we had gotten to where we were headed I felt terribly lonely and alone. I wrapped my arms around myself.

"What beverages are you offering?"

"No more beverages," I said.

"Jack Daniels?" Chuck had some under the sink. Derek Head looked me up and down. "You're *fine*, Fiona."

"You're not bad yourself." I burped and then he did. We threw on our clothes and went downstairs to the kitchen, where under the sink was a bottle of Jack Daniels. "Here," I said, pushing him toward the back door.

I walked into the hall and saw that Frankie's bedroom door was shut. I waited and knocked. "Good God," I heard my brother-in-law whisper. I teetered on the carpet, letting the situation swish around my brain. Meanwhile my date whizzed past me, flying into the bathroom, guided by some inner antennae. I heard him heave into the toilet, spewing those fine appetizers. My stricken, hairy brother-in-law opened the door, standing in his boxers and socks.

"Where is she?" I said, darting into the room. Constance Poblanski was behind the door, buttoning up.

"This isn't exactly what it looks like, even though it's bad," Chuck said.

Derek Head spewed some more and flushed.

"Quit flushing, it's gonna back up," I yelled. "You, Chuck, have children sleeping upstairs."

"They sleep like the dead," he barely said.

"And no money for you," I said to Constance Poblanski, corrupted babysitter. I jerked her into the hall.

Chuck slid into his pants. "No, wait," he said, reaching for his wallet. He handed her a ten.

"You must never, ever speak of this." I grabbed her wrist. "Never. Understand?"

"I'm not an idiot," she said.

"Yes, you are."

"I am," Chuck said, looking beat and sick. There was more heaving, a wretched noise, and more flushing and finally a watery froth spilled under the door.

"Quit the fucking flushing, you moron," I said.

"I want this bra," Constance said, reaching into Frankie's laundry basket.

"Like hell!" I said.

She turned to me. "I'm not going to say anything." And she grabbed her see-through purse and walked out into the night.

"Chuck, Chuck," I wailed. "You dog!"

"Look, Fiona, my ride drops me off. I come in and find her parading around our bedroom in Frankie's bra. 'I didn't hear you come in,' she tells me. She takes it off right in front of me." Chuck looked at me with drowning eyes. "We didn't do it," he whispered. "I wanted to see if I could…"

"*Chuck*?" I sang.

"Frankie's so hard…" He looked like he might cry.

Derek Head swung open the bathroom door, "Fine Fiona, I am in trouble." He was dabbled with puke.

"Good grief!" Chuck said.

I ran outside and caught up with Constance, who was headed for the Anderson house, where presumably Laura Rossi was babysitting. I reached into my pocketbook and took a handful of that disability money and thrust it at her. "Make it so you go to the Andersons' from now on and Laura comes here. Can you do that?" She brushed the money away. I pressed it into her hand.

"All right," she said in a little-girl voice. But I couldn't protect my sister. Frankie was in for a fall. There wasn't anything for me to do. Frankie needed to change and accept her life; it was a good life. I walked away, feeling sober and strangely calm.

Inside, Chuck had coffee going and had set the kids' throw-up bowl next to Derek Head. Derek was cleaned up—except for his wet sludgy knees—and sitting at the table with his head in his hands. Chuck was telling Derek Head to drink lots of water and do a shot of Nyquil before bed. I'd never not told Frankie anything. But I wouldn't turn in Chuck.

How strange it would feel to hold such a big secret.

Several cups of coffee later, Chuck gave me his keys and I drove Derek Head to the Chowder Pot, where he lay down on his couch. I fished in his pocket for the key and took out his blanket and pillow and tucked him in. "Give me a kiss, Fioner," he slurred. The smell wasn't good, and I patted his shoulder.

I sat there for a moment, watching Lord and Lady Anderson rise to leave. The dark, smoky room had pretty much cleared out and was littered with empty glasses, dirty plates, and butt marks on the soft couches. The Andersons looked tired and a bit disheveled, and they walked in single file toward the exit. Regular folks. I felt sticky and forlorn.

"Derek," I whispered, suddenly. I didn't quite believe what I was seeing. "Open your eyes. Isn't that the thief from Wawa? On the love seat?"

Derek opened his sleepy eyes and yawned pukey air at me. He nodded and then snuggled up on his pillow, licking his lips.

I called Chuck from a pay phone downstairs, and while I was filling him in, the thief walked down the stairs and right past me. I told Chuck the guy was leaving, and Chuck said he'd have someone at the Chowder Pot lickety-split. "Trust me, Fiona," he said. I did.

I sat at the bar and took out one of my crisp disability fifties and ordered a Bailey's Irish Cream. I wasn't exactly happy—and it was certainly true that everything was a mess—but even still, sitting there in the bar I felt a kind of thaw happening, as if shoots were pushing through the cool ground, little green tendrils, insistent and inevitable.

I had to go back to Manhattan—back to my third-floor walk-up on Cherry Lane and back to member services at Wildlife of America. I would keep some of my old friends—the friends who'd checked in on me, the friend who'd mailed me a post-card on which he had given the Statue of Liberty a pair of binoculars and written, "See you soon?" I'd let Mr. Snodgrass fix me up with his veterinarian nephew. I was beginning to long for the city with all its noise and hazards and surprises.

Two squad cars sat outside the Chowder Pot, flashing their red lights. The thief—in handcuffs—was pushed into the backseat of one of the cars while Lord and Lady Anderson stood in the headlights, the red siren lights whirling across their faces. The smell of pot hung in the air. "They were only smoking a joint, for godsakes," a waitress said to me. Our noble Lord and Lady liked to smoke weed! I couldn't help but smile, though I felt badly, too; they looked so damn mortified standing there with the cops. It was hard to imagine they'd spend the night in the slammer.

Frankie had probably returned home from her evening-of-beauty. I wondered what it was like, all that dipping, sanding, and steam cleaning. I pictured her pink and tender, momentarily blissful. Walking along the sidewalk toward the car, I wondered if I was betraying Frankie by keeping Chuck's secret, and I honestly didn't know the answer. There wasn't much to feel good about, and yet I did know one thing: Frankie would love hearing the latest evolution in the Lord and Lady Anderson saga. One last tale for the road, and then we both needed to get a move on.

ACKNOWLEDGMENTS

Bighearted thanks to all the good people along the way who helped with these stories, especially Sue Collard, Sara Eckel, Shelley Griffin, Cara Kaiser, Nancy Ludmerer, and Bob Schirmer. So many thanks to my parents for their support and encouragement. Special thanks to The Writers Community, the New York Mills Arts Retreat, and the Jerome Foundation. Thanks also to Tom Vinges for his enthusiastic reads of the early drafts and lending me the laptop. And endless thanks to Tina Bennett and Anika Streitfeld for their commitment to this book.